THE HIGH TRAIL

Demoted and disgraced, Lieutenant Calvin Glaze is offered a chance of redemption: leading a patrol through the mountain passes up to Hunger Flats, to track down the hideout of the Crowley Gang. Assigned an elderly cook-house private, a one-legged sergeant, and two soldiers up on charges, Glaze has private doubts about his patrol's likely efficacy. Three weeks later, on the treacherous High Trail — with the supply wagon lost, his men mutinous, and harsh weather closing in — he begins to suspect his mission was designed to fail from the start . . .

✝ R.C   MUN

SPECIAL MESSAGE TO READERS

THE ULVERSCROFT FOUNDATION
(registered UK charity number 264873)

was established in 1972 to provide funds for research, diagnosis and treatment of eye diseases.
Examples of major projects funded by the Ulverscroft Foundation are:-

- The Children's Eye Unit at Moorfields Eye Hospital, London
- The Ulverscroft Children's Eye Unit at Great Ormond Street Hospital for Sick Children
- Funding research into eye diseases and treatment at the Department of Ophthalmology, University of Leicester
- The Ulverscroft Vision Research Group, Institute of Child Health
- Twin operating theatres at the Western Ophthalmic Hospital, London
- The Chair of Ophthalmology at the Royal Australian College of Ophthalmologists

You can help further the work of the Foundation by making a donation or leaving a legacy.
Every contribution is gratefully received. If you would like to help support the Foundation or require further information, please contact:

THE ULVERSCROFT FOUNDATION
The Green, Bradgate Road, Anstey
Leicester LE7 7FU, England
Tel: (0116) 236 4325

website: www.foundation.ulverscroft.co

ROB HILL

THE HIGH TRAIL

Complete and Unabridged

LINFORD
Leicester

First published in Great Britain in 2013 by
Robert Hale Limited
London

First Linford Edition
published 2015
by arrangement with
Robert Hale Limited
London

A catalogue record for this book is available
from the British Library.

ISBN 978–1–4448–2500–8

Published by
F. A. Thorpe (Publishing)
Anstey, Leicestershire

Set by Words & Graphics Ltd.
Anstey, Leicestershire
Printed and bound in Great Britain by
T. J. International Ltd., Padstow, Cornwall

This book is printed on acid-free paper

1

With a critical eye, Colonel Bolt stood at the Command Room window and watched the regiment fall in for roll call. It was hardly necessary to begin the day this early but Bolt prided himself on being a stickler. He nodded in approval as the drill sergeants barked their commands. He wanted the men to know who was in charge from the moment they opened their eyes.

Frost on the morning air indicated a change of season. Summer had gone. Grey dawn light revealed the open plains, which stretched for a thousand miles east of Fort Brandish and the wall of mountain that reared to the west. Erosion scored the lower slopes, while sugar pines and blue cone cedars hid the steep-sided ravines. Above the tree line, mist cloaked the peaks, which the colonel guessed were already covered with snow.

Lieutenant Calvin Glaze stared at the colonel's rigid back. He had been summoned, stood at ease and made to wait. Unable to gauge the colonel's mood, Glaze was on edge; he had had run-ins with his commanding officer before. Bolt did not suffer fools. When the colonel turned and gestured Glaze to sit, Glaze was relieved to see a tight, satisfied smile on his face; the fall-in must have gone well.

The lieutenant brought up a stiff-backed chair while the hard-bitten old cavalryman perched above him on the edge of his desk like a hawk about to swoop. The colonel's dark eyes glittered; his fierce nose and chiseled cheeks were carved above the steel grey moustache as thick as a yard broom, which hid his mouth. Glaze looked up hoping that the expression of earnest seriousness he fixed on his face would not make him appear sullen; he wished the colonel to think him the most willing soldier under his command.

The colonel took a second to study the young officer in front of him. His eyes instinctively swept over his uniform in search of a speck of dust on the jacket, a crease that was less than blade sharp or a button that might not shine like the sun. He found none of these. Nevertheless, Bolt was contemptuous of Glaze and the training academy recommendations he had brought with him early in the summer. From the colonel's point of view, the few short months of Glaze's posting had been a disaster. The lieutenant's sweep of blond hair, his blue eyes and open, smiling face might appeal to the ladies in Boston salons, he judged, but as far as Bolt himself was concerned, they counted for nothing.

'Lieutenant Glaze,' the colonel began. 'Calvin.'

It was the first time the colonel had used his Christian name. Glaze felt a blush of pleasure rise to his cheek; at the same time, unease twisted within him. The colonel's sharp eyes seemed able to penetrate his thoughts.

Despite himself, Glaze raised his chin a fraction. His back was poker straight and his hands were loosely clasped in his lap. He wanted the colonel to notice the formality of the way he sat; he wanted him to see attentiveness in his face. Outside, the sergeants yelped commands.

'Got a mission for you, Calvin.'

Colonel Bolt had used his name for a second time. Glaze swallowed. Suddenly his throat felt dry. 'Sir?'

'I want you to lead a patrol up to Hunger Flats to find out where the Crowley Gang is holed up.'

Glaze heard the word 'lead'. The colonel had said he wanted him to lead. He felt blood rush in his head; he felt the muscles of his face move into a smile, which he fought to control in case it made him look like an idiot. The colonel's eyes bored into him.

'I know you want to make captain again,' Bolt went on. 'This could be your chance.'

4

This was too much. Promotion. He could write to Charlotte. Glaze held his expression in place like a mask. The only sign of his excitement was a movement of his hands in his lap; he clasped them briefly and then released them again.

The colonel pushed himself off the desk and made a small jump on to the floor. The thud of his boot heels against the boards made Glaze's heart miss a beat.

'Wagon trains have been attacked all summer,' Bolt said. 'Every time I send my men out, the Crowleys disappear like smoke on a breeze.'

He looked down at Glaze and spoke quietly as though he was taking him into a confidence.

'Problem is,' Bolt said, 'whenever we send a division up to look for them, they see us coming and skedaddle. But if we found out where these fellas are holed up, we could send our boys right in after them.'

Glaze felt that the colonel was

sharing with him decisions of leadership on which the success of the regiment depended. He nodded to show he followed, even though he still could not quite be sure what Bolt had in mind.

'This is where you come in,' Bolt continued.

'I want you to take a sergeant and a couple of men. Sergeant Carey hasn't been out on patrol for a while; he's reliable. Take Privates Miller and Schmidt along, too. You'll need supplies for a month and someone to take care of 'em so take Private Cobb, he's a fine trail cook. He can drive the chuck wagon.'

Bolt's face darkened.

'You know what happened to the Weaver party, don't you?'

'Sir, that's hardly likely to . . . ' Glaze began.

The bones of the Weaver family had been found in one of the high passes early in spring. Cut off by the winter snows and having suffered for weeks without food, they burned their wagons and ate their mules. Cobb had the reputation of being the best cook in the fort; the colonel was making sure they were looked after.

'Take the High Trail. If the Crowleys are up there, they won't expect you to come that way; everyone takes the route the wagons use now. Folks say it's a hard ride but I rode that route myself; a young officer like you won't have trouble getting through. Soon as you find out where their camp is, head straight back here. Then we can think about the best way to get a unit up to tackle 'em.'

Strategy, Glaze thought. The colonel was going to involve him in deciding on strategy. He clasped his hands, unclasped them and pressed his palms down on his thighs to stop himself fidgeting.

Then another thought came to him. The men. Sergeant Carey had been wounded at Buzzard Creek, hadn't he? Why had Bolt suggested him? The names of the two privates didn't ring any bells. A mission like this needed soldiers who were experienced in the mountains. Why shouldn't he pick his own men? He could think of the names of a dozen who were suited.

'It was unfortunate that the incident on the plains took place so soon after you were posted here.' The colonel's voice rasped like a file. 'We both know why I had to demote you. We both understand that.'

Glaze felt hot inside his uniform. His collar was too tight.

Bolt strode over to the window and spoke to the view across the parade ground where the regiment awaited his inspection.

'This is your chance to get your rank back, Calvin. This is your chance to redeem yourself. Because as things stand, your reputation . . . ' The colonel's words faded away; his attention was taken up by the lines of men outside. 'What every man does affects the morale of the regiment.'

Glaze concentrated on keeping his hands still. Bolt turned to him, looking for agreement.

'You know what I'm talking about?'

'Sir,' Glaze said; there was lead in his belly.

He could suggest that the choice of men wasn't suitable. He could say that they were only experienced in plains fighting, that they were unused to the mountains. He could ask to be allowed to select men who had already been on patrol in the foothills. When he looked up, Bolt was still staring out of the window.

'Ain't pretending it'll be easy,' the colonel said. 'Cold nights at this time of year.'

Bolt glanced at Glaze to see how he was taking all this.

'The High Trail leads right up to Hunger Flats,' the colonel continued. 'That's where each wagon train leaves supplies under a cairn for whoever comes up after them. If you've got any spare when you're up there, you can add it to what's under the stones.'

'Sir.'

Glaze could say that the men weren't right for the mission, that there were others better suited. He moved his fingers under his palms until they were clenched like fists.

'I need a precise position of the Crowley camp.' Bolt fixed Glaze with a hard stare. 'Routes in and out, where their lookouts are, how we can best make an attack.' He chuckled to himself. 'They won't be expecting us to come looking for them this late in the season. We got surprise on our side.' He lowered his voice. 'I'm counting on you, Calvin. If this is successful, I'll have all the reason I need to bump you up to captain again.'

Glaze swallowed; he knew he was blushing. The serge collar scraped his throat; sweat pricked the back of his neck.

'Won't let you down, sir,' he said. His stomach still felt like lead.

'One more thing.' Bolt slid open a

drawer in his desk. 'Charlotte asked me to give you this. The day she left for Boston, you were out on patrol.'

Unsmiling, he handed Glaze a sealed envelope inscribed with his name. Glaze's heart skipped at the sight of Charlotte's neat copperplate.

'Gave her my word I'd pass it on to you,' Bolt said coldly. 'Now I have.'

Glaze's hand shook slightly. Sealed with a blob of red wax, the vellum felt warm to the touch. He longed to slit the envelope open; Charlotte's words waited for him inside.

'Of course,' the colonel announced, 'this marks the end of your friendship.' He hesitated as if the word tasted bad. He stared at Glaze, daring him to contradict. 'I made that clear to my daughter before she left.'

'Sir . . . ?' Glaze began.

'Subject's closed.' Bolt rounded on him. 'I've put you in charge of a mission. I've given you a chance to recover your reputation.' His eyes narrowed. 'You've got a day to make

11

your arrangements. Update my second-in-command, Major Fairburn, this evening. Leave at first light tomorrow.'

As Colonel Bolt swept through the Command Room door, a drill sergeant's yelp brought the men to attention. Glaze saluted, followed the colonel out into the cold morning air and took his place in the parade.

Privately, Bolt congratulated himself on his tactics. His plan to track down the Crowleys this late in the season was something that would cause nods of approval at headquarters. No commander had tried sending out a search party quickly followed by a band of troopers. Even though the gang was troublesome, it was not particularly well armed; tracking it down was the problem. Bolt knew he had nothing to lose. Even if the mission failed to pinpoint a hideout, his initiative would be noted.

Then there was the personal matter. By putting Lieutenant Glaze in charge, Bolt provided himself with the ideal opportunity to promote him and recommend him for transfer. It was the easiest way to get rid of him. The colonel couldn't wait to see the back of him; the man was a presumptuous upstart and probably a coward to boot.

Within days of being posted to the fort as a newly appointed captain, Glaze had turned his first routine patrol into a disaster in which a handful of Sioux braves massacred every man. Somehow Glaze himself got away unscathed. He claimed the war party had let him live to witness the atrocity and he came back with some story about the attack being a reprisal for the murder of a chief's daughter. Bolt had hardly bothered to listen; even now, he doubted that he had got to the bottom of what happened. When news of the tragedy got out back at the fort, morale nosedived. An officer who came back without his men? The colonel demoted Glaze on the spot.

As if this wasn't enough, Bolt's 17-year-old daughter, Charlotte, had the audacity to announce that she had come to what she called 'an understanding' with Glaze. Bolt had arranged for Charlotte to spend the summer at Fort Brandish and Glaze had been part of the escort he sent to accompany her along the last hundred miles of the trail. Charlotte made this ridiculous announcement within days of her arrival, shortly before the incident that caused Glaze's demotion.

From past experience, the colonel knew that if he forbade the relationship outright, he would simply open the door to weeks of petulant histrionics from his daughter. He had to walk on eggshells. The best thing he could do was to quietly let Charlotte know that Glaze had been demoted and manoeuvre him out of the way.

Now that he had dealt with Glaze, there was one other thing on the colonel's mind that morning. He wanted to get the inspection over with as soon as possible and call in at the stables to check on the fine young stallion he had earmarked for himself. The horse immediately caught his eye when a group of itinerant traders brought a herd into the fort. Fiery and dominant amongst the other horses, he was strong and a good runner. Bolt couldn't wait to put him through his paces outside the stockade. Mightily proud of his reputation as a horseman, this was the kind of challenge he relished. He smiled to himself. There wasn't a stallion to get the better of him yet.

On the parade ground, the colonel went through the morning notices quickly. Glaze's heart raced when Bolt announced his name as being in command of the search party to track down the Crowleys. As soon as the regiment was dismissed, he would find Sergeant Carey and get him to call the men together.

2

Built on the site of an old meeting point where trappers brought their pelts down from the mountains, Fort Brandish was the westernmost stockade on the Oregon Trail. In the early days, it was a peaceful place where parties of Paiute would ride in to exchange deer hides for food. The army took over as a response to calls for protection from the pioneers, who worried about attacks from the Sioux and felt threatened by the charlatans who ran the trading posts.

The season for wagon trains was at an end. The band of Lakota Sioux who had been in the area all summer had departed. There was talk of trouble further south and last week the first unit had been redeployed; Bolt had made sure that they provided a suitable escort for Charlotte, who he had dispatched back to her aunt in Boston. Over the next few weeks, other units would also be posted. Within a month, the first snows would arrive and the skeleton force retained at Brandish would hunker down, sit out the winter and wait to be relieved in the spring.

While Glaze waited for Sergeant Carey outside the stores, he slid the letter out of the inside pocket of his uniform. There was his name in Charlotte's flawless script. He turned it over and ran his finger over the blood-coloured sealing wax. He was tempted to open it right then and there. He looked up and scanned the parade ground; the door to the stores was still closed. Still no sign of Carey.

'Of course, this is the end of your friendship.' As Glaze pictured the colonel's unsmiling face, his words clanged inside his head. It was the demotion. Bolt still blamed him for the loss of his men on the plains yet he was giving him a chance to redeem himself. Maybe he didn't think so badly of him after all. Glaze couldn't make sense of it.

Glaze slipped his finger under the fold of the envelope and prised the seal away. He hadn't meant to open it here on the parade ground but he couldn't help it. He had intended to save it until he found some private corner of the Officers' Mess where he would have the chance to savour every word. But his hands knew what he really wanted. They took on a life of their own; he watched them slip the folded paper out of the envelope and flatten it along the crease for him to read. As the words danced in front of his eyes, he realized that his hand was shaking.

'My dear Calvin, As you are out on a patrol today, I shall not be able to see you to say goodbye . . . '

Glaze looked up, just to check that no one was watching him.

' . . . I should have been especially

grateful to see you in person as my papa has forbidden the continuance of our friendship and was most vehement in doing so. I understand neither the reason for this nor why he has waited to break this news to me on the day I am due to set out for Boston and can only suppose, as always, that he is acting for the best. In fact, I had to plead with him for permission to be allowed to write to you at all . . . '

A shout from somewhere broke into Glaze's reverie.

'Lieutenant.'

'My father also reiterated to me the most distressing news of your demotion in rank and became most perturbed and angry when I said you had already made me aware of this. His account of the reason for this drastic action differed so wildly from the account you gave me that I am practically torn in two. I would give *anything to be allowed an opportunity to talk this over with you face to face. My poor papa heaped blame upon you most mercilessly and talked at great length about the reputation of the regiment, how he has sacrificed his own career upon that particular altar and how I could never understand the relinquishments and denials he has made . . .* '

'Lieutenant.' It was Carey's cheerful sing-song voice.

Glaze looked up, quickly folded the letter and slipped it back inside his jacket.

A red-faced Sergeant Carey hurried awkwardly towards him; his peg leg jabbed the parade ground dirt. Even though he liked Carey, Glaze felt awkward; each time he had to deal with the other ranks, his demotion from captain to lieutenant weighed on his shoulders like a yoke.

But with thoughts of the mission in his head, Glaze heard Colonel Bolt say the word 'lead' again; he made himself focus.

Carey arrived breathless and listened intently as Glaze gave an outline of Bolt's instructions.

'The colonel asked for me?' Carey seemed astonished.

Sergeant Carey held a clipboard and the day's duty roster in his hand.

'I ain't been out on patrol since Buzzard Creek.'

Carey looked down at his wooden leg.

'Don't get me wrong, Lieutenant,' he said fiercely, 'I can still ride. It's just that they put me in charge here and no one's asked me.'

'Reckon the colonel thinks it's your turn,' Glaze said.

Carey was a tough, short, square-built man. Ever since joining the Mounted Rifles as a boy, the army had been his life. He had been part of the detail that built forts all along the Emigrant Road and had survived numerous skirmishes with the Sioux.

Since the Buzzard Creek incident when three arrows smashed the bones in his right leg and the regiment's sawbones had to amputate, he had been assigned quartermaster's duties.

Able to keep up a good pace on his false leg, and because of his resolute good spirits, Carey was a popular figure round the fort. None of the men had forgotten what a tough fighter he had been; the stories of how he had taken part in charge after charge with three arrows sticking out of his leg were part of legend. As far as the officers were concerned, his intense loyalty to the regiment and the way he handled the men earned him their respect.

As Fort Brandish went about its morning duties, the main expanse of the parade ground was temporarily abandoned. Smoke rose from the forge in the eastern corner; a group of men assembled by the main gate ready for drill; sentries kept watch from their platforms. Overhead, the sky was steel grey and clouds promised rain.

'Walk with me, Sergeant,' Glaze said.

As the two men headed out to the perimeter, the slow clang of a blacksmith's hammer echoed across the parade ground like a knell. A drill sergeant screamed at the line of men by the gate.

Glaze walked with his hands clasped behind his back. He was taller than the sergeant and his leisurely stride meant that Carey had to move quickly to keep up. Glaze looked straight ahead as he outlined the colonel's plan; hobbling along half a pace behind, Carey drank in every word.

'Supplies for a month,' Carey said. 'That means more than one mule.'

'The colonel specifically said a wagon,' Glaze said.

'High Trail's too narrow for a chow wagon, ain't it?' Carey looked worried. 'Anyhow, won't the turnaround take longer than a month?'

'Colonel's rode the trail himself,' Glaze said. 'Reckons we'll have enough supplies to leave some at the cairn up on the flats.'

'How many men?' Carey said.

'Us, Miller and Schmidt.' Glaze looked straight ahead. 'And a cook.'

He waited for Carey to comment on the names of the men. As the sergeants at Fort Brandish knew the men well, the officers often left them to select their own personnel for specific duties. This was why Glaze had been puzzled that Bolt had nominated each member of the patrol. While Carey was silent, Glaze quickened his pace so the sergeant had to hurry.

'I assume they're fit,' Glaze prompted.

'They're on charges in the lock-up,' Carey said. 'Due to be released this morning.'

Glaze halted sharply and turned to stare at the sergeant. He gripped his hands tight behind his back.

'What charges?'

'Miller got into a brawl and laid another man out cold. Schmidt was caught stealing from the kitchens.'

Carey looked Glaze in the eye. 'They're good soldiers, Lieutenant. They just get themselves into trouble from time to time.'

Glaze nodded briefly. A line of sweat pricked inside his collar again. Why hadn't Colonel Bolt suggested he or Carey choose the men? Why had he named two men who were up on charges?

'Schmidt is the strongest man stationed out here,' Carey went on. 'Ought to be, he eats enough for four of 'em.'

Carey was proud of the men; Glaze could hear it in his voice. All the sergeants were. Then Glaze remembered Schmidt. Built like a mountain, he was the regiment's wrestling champion; he wasn't the brightest but he obeyed orders to the letter.

'The wrestler,' Glaze said.

Carey grinned. For a moment, Glaze thought Carey was going to launch into a story about some feat of strength Schmidt had carried out and cut him short.

'Miller?'

'Always the first to volunteer.' There was loyalty in Glaze's eye. 'Always wants to ride point.'

'Reliable?' Glaze said.

'Tough fighter,' Carey said. 'Kinda got a short fuse, that's why he gets hauled up on charges. Face to face with danger in the field, he's fearless. You can rely on him, Lieutenant, no question.'

'The colonel wants Private Cobb to take charge of the chow wagon,' Glaze added confidently.

Carey laughed aloud at the mention of Cobb's name. Newt Cobb was the oldest man stationed at Brandish. He had lived west of the Missouri longer than any of them; he told stories about the early days, which made the young troopers' hair stand on end. Having spent his whole career in the cook-house, everyone knew him.

'Newt ain't a young man, Lieutenant,' Carey said. 'He'll find the going hard. Ain't there someone else?'

'Colonel mentioned Cobb by name,' Glaze said. His collar felt tight again. 'Anyhow, he'll be driving the wagon.'

Carey nodded. If he disagreed with the order, he didn't show it.

'Besides that, he's the best cook we got,' Glaze added. 'Must mean the colonel wants us all kept well fed.'

'Guess so, Lieutenant,' Carey grinned amiably. 'Tell you one thing, I never reckoned me and old Newt would be going out on patrol together. Thought them days had long gone.'

'Round up the men, Sergeant. Briefing in one hour.'

3

Three Weeks Later.

Private Newton Cobb's broken body lay spread-eagled across rocks at the bottom of the ravine. His limbs were awkwardly twisted and he was still. The bodies of two pack mules and smashed remains of a supply wagon littered the ground around him. There was no movement from one of the mules but the second twisted in its harness in an effort to struggle to its feet. It was clearly in agony but any sound it made was drowned out by the explosion of white water, which cannoned close by.

A hundred feet above and hanging back from the place where the path had given way, the men stared down in horror. There were no outcrops, no hand holds, nothing to break a fall. Loose scree from the most recent landslide balanced above Cobb's body; the slightest disturbance would bury him.

'Was he riding?' Glaze snapped. 'I gave the order to lead the animals.'

Carey pulled a Winchester out of his saddle holster.

'What are you doing?' Glaze's face was white.

Carey fired twice; the rifle shots pierced the thunder of the river. Both mules. Accurate head shots. As it was the end of summer, the flow, though fast, was diminished. If it had been spring when the ravine was a conduit for thawing snow, Cobb's body, the wagon and the carcasses of the mules would have been swept away in seconds.

Carey let his eyes rest on the bodies of the animals far below him and tried to detect any sign of movement before he holstered his rifle. Schmidt held his own and Carey's horse while he took the shots. Shock rooted the big man to the spot; keeping back from the edge, he craned over the sergeant's shoulder to get a better view.

'I told him to climb down and lead the mules,' Glaze said. 'I gave the order.'

He tightened his grip on the bridle of his horse and looked to Carey for confirmation but the sergeant was concentrating on the animals below and seemed not to have heard.

'Reckon Newt's dead, Sarge?' Schmidt's voice shook.

There was a shout further up the track, the sound of running feet. Miller had been up ahead on point; he charged towards them, his army issue Colt in his hand.

'Heard shots.' Miller caught his breath. 'What are you shooting at, Sarge?'

'You're supposed to be keeping lookout,' Glaze said.

'Ain't seen nothing because there's nothing to see,' Miller snapped. 'No one in their right mind comes along here.'

Glaze caught his eye. Was that deliberate insolence? He let it go.

Then Miller caught sight of Cobb's body and the dead mules far below them; he saw the rifle in Carey's hands. A few yards back along the track he saw where a weakness in the rock had given way and taken a wide bite out of the path.

'Sure won't be going back this way. Wagon took the whole path with it.' Miller looked from Schmidt to Carey. 'Who's going down to check on Newt?'

The question hung between them for a moment. In both their faces, he saw shock, fear and gratitude it wasn't them lying down there across the rocks. Last of all he looked at Glaze. He was holding the bridle of his horse too tight.

'Lieutenant?'

'He's dead,' Glaze said. 'No one could survive that. Besides, it's too steep. Even if we got down there, we couldn't get back up again.'

'You're just going to leave him?'

As Glaze stared down into the ravine

at the bodies, the broken carcass of the wagon and the supplies scattered over the rocks, the rumble of the white water pounded in his head. The eyes of the men were on him; he felt sweat prick his neck.

'Best get the horses off this stretch,' Glaze said.

Miller was behind him. Schmidt and Carey followed in single file.

Glaze led them for a mile up the steep climb until he found a place where the snaking path widened. Years before, some avalanche had torn away an outcrop of rock and left a flat ledge wide enough for the horses to stand and the men to sit and rest under the shelter of a wide overhang. It was a barren place; there was no topsoil and only groundsel and clumps of vetch clung tenaciously to the fissures in the rock. From up here, the sound of the river charging down the gutter of the ravine was faint.

Heavy grey clouds loomed overhead

and covered the peaks. Cold air bit through the men's clothes. Miller inspected the lip of the path and the drop below.

'We could get down here.'

'Too steep.' Glaze stood behind him stared down into the ravine. 'We'd break our legs.'

'What about Newt?' Miller said.

Glaze saw Miller's hands ball into fists by his sides.

'What about him?' Glaze said.

Miller appealed to Carey for support. 'We can't just leave him.'

'He's dead, Miller.' Glaze felt the muscles in his shoulders stiffen.

'We got to make sure, ain't we?' Miller looked from Glaze to Sergeant Carey.

'We'll rest here awhile,' Glaze cut across him. 'Then we'll press on.'

He turned to stare up the track; Miller choked back a protest.

'Sarge,' Miller appealed to Carey. 'You reckon we should leave Newt for the buzzards?'

'You heard the lieutenant,' Carey snapped.

Glaze had his back to the men. He patted the neck of his horse and made a show of checking the bridle.

'That's Newt down there, Sarge.' Pity tore Miller's voice. 'We can't just leave him. We got to see if he's alive.'

'You heard,' Carey said but he spoke quietly this time, less sure.

'What about you?' Miller barked at Schmidt. 'You want to leave Newt so the crows can peck out his eyes?'

Worry crumpled the big man's face; he looked to Carey for an answer.

'All the supplies are down there,' Miller continued. 'We won't have nothing to eat unless we get down there.'

'That's it.' Carey's face darkened. 'You heard what's been said.' He turned to Schmidt. 'You stay out of this.'

'I heard,' Miller said. 'I just ain't about to leave Newt without knowing if he's dead or alive.'

34

Right in front of them, Miller dropped to his knees and let himself down over the edge of the path. Scree tumbled ahead of him as he struggled for each foothold. Carey's shouts echoed over his head. He pressed himself flat against the rock, hands grasping for anything to prevent himself from falling. Glaze joined the others and peered down; his fists were clenched, his face a mask.

Miller heard Carey's voice scream something about being on a charge when he got back but he wasn't listening. He inched his way down the cliff side, foot hold to hand hold; at times he thought the bones in his fingers would crack. Loose stones rattled ahead of him; roots of shrubs came away in his hands. When his feet failed to find a resting place, he slid and the rock face tore his clothes.

Glaze left the others peering over the edge and found a place to lean back against the rock on the far side of the ledge. Tiredness soaked through his aching limbs; he was glad of a respite from the climb and that there was nothing to do while they waited for Miller. He felt inside his jacket, took out a letter and began to read. He handled the pages carefully; the paper was weak from being folded and refolded so many times. Glaze quickly became absorbed. When he looked up, Schmidt and Sergeant Carey were waiting for him.

'News, Sergeant?' Glaze said.

He folded the pages and slipped them under his jacket. Carey was used to this; the lieutenant stared at that letter every chance he got.

'Got down to the river,' Carey said. 'He's working his way downstream.'

'Good,' Glaze said. He stood up. 'You and I should walk back down the track and keep parallel with him. Schmidt can stay here with the horses.'

He knew Carey was going to say that left no one on point.

'Schmidt can keep lookout at the same time.'

The sergeant nodded.

'We haven't seen anyone since we left the fort,' Glaze added, though he hardly needed to explain.

Carey clearly wanted to talk to him and Glaze could guess what he was likely to say. He would be worried about the supplies; he would want to know what to do about Miller disobeying a direct order. And then he would be concerned that they had been in the mountains for almost three weeks without seeing a soul, let alone one of the Crowleys. He would want to know how much further Glaze intended to take them.

A couple of days, Glaze judged, and they would reach Hunger Flats, the plateau where wagon trains rested up before making a final push to the high passes, the place where the food cairn was.

As an afterthought, Glaze unhitched his canteen from his saddle and slung it over his shoulder. It was not that he didn't trust Schmidt particularly but all the water they had was in their canteens. Glaze was on his guard; he didn't want to put temptation in Schmidt's path.

'Take your canteen, Sergeant.'

Carey looked surprised.

Best not to make an issue of Miller's blatant disregard of his authority right now, Glaze reflected. Carey might bluster and want the private taken to task but Miller would expect to be on a charge; the sergeant could let him know that this would happen when they got back to the fort.

Glaze headed back down the track with Carey following behind. Even going downhill progress was slow; they stepped on loose stones, which could cause them to miss their footing. Carey's peg leg clicked on the rock path and the pebbles made him lurch; every now and again, he knocked fragments of rock over the edge. The two men were forced to stay tight to the rock wall whenever the track narrowed and the twists and turns obscured any sight of Miller on the valley floor below.

After a while it became clear that even though Miller had to pick his way between boulders, the path by the river was more direct; he was making faster progress than they were. Glaze quickened his pace. He could hear Carey's short breaths behind him as he struggled to keep up.

Within an hour, they were back at the place where Cobb had fallen. The break in the rock was sharp-edged; the unweathered strata, which lay beneath the path, glittered. The men kept back from it; suddenly the path where they stood seemed less safe than before. The roar of white water filled the valley again.

Glaze and Carey approached the edge of the path. In the midst of the bedlam of the animal corpses and the broken wagon, they saw Miller bending over Cobb.

'Is he alive?' Carey breathed.

Glaze stiffened; he clutched the sergeant's arm to steady himself as he took another step towards the edge. Miller's back was turned towards them.

'Can't be,' Glaze said. The sound of the white water filled his head.

'What's Miller doing?' Carey said.

Glaze didn't answer. The question irritated him. How could he tell? How could either of them? His thoughts started to burn. He hadn't stopped Miller from going down there. If Cobb was alive, maybe that wouldn't be good enough. Maybe Bolt would expect him to have led them all down there; he would have expected some kind of rescue mission. He tightened his grip on Carey's arm. If Cobb had survived, he should have organized the men to bring him back up. Glaze began to feel hot under his clothes; his back prickled with sweat.

Still with his back to them, Miller stood up. He must know they were watching. Why hadn't he turned round? He knew they wanted to see Cobb. Was he blocking their view on purpose? Glaze felt a line of sweat on his neck even though the air was cold.

Miller stepped aside. Cobb still lay there; something was different but Glaze couldn't tell what it was. Miller climbed over the rocks to one of the mules and started to unlash a pack of supplies. Cobb was dead and Miller was taking whatever he could carry. That must be it. But Glaze still wasn't sure. The cold air made him shiver.

Miller unpacked something and then started to search the river-bank. They watched him gather an armful of sticks and set about lighting a fire. He kept looking across at Cobb. Was he talking to him? Still Miller did not look up. Maybe this wasn't insolence; maybe he just hadn't realized they were there. If they called out, their word would be drowned by the sound of the water. Down where Miller was the bombardment would be deafening.

Blue smoke curled up from Miller's fire. They watched him sit down beside it. He was cooking something. Making coffee, maybe. Glaze became aware of the hunger gnawing his own belly. He hadn't eaten since first light. Didn't Miller realize they needed food, too? Maybe they should have all gone down there. It was a hard climb but at least they would have been able to feed themselves.

'How's he gonna get back up,' Carey said suddenly, 'if he's carrying supplies?'

Glaze stared down at Miller hunched over the fire. He didn't seem to be talking to Cobb any more; he wasn't looking at him.

'He won't need to bring much,' Glaze said. 'We're only a day or so from the cairn.'

Carey looked uncertain.

'Pemmican, hard tack all sealed up,' Glaze said. 'I'd lay money there's coffee there, too. Each train that comes through takes what they need and leaves something in exchange.'

'If it's a day's ride, the sooner Miller gets back up here the better,' Carey said. He stepped back from the edge and turned to Glaze. 'You want me to put him on a charge right now?'

'Warn him,' Glaze said. 'I'll deal with it back at Brandish. For now we'll just concentrate on the mission. Another few days and we'll have to turn back anyway.'

Carey was relieved. He sat down on the path and leaned back against the rock wall. He reached inside his jacket and offered his tobacco to Glaze. Glaze was wrong-footed by this act of friendship from his sergeant. He shook his head.

'Don't use it,' he said. 'My fiancée —'

A blush crept up his face as he realized he had said too much. Carey waited for him to finish. Glaze gave a little laugh in his throat to show that it was nothing and he wasn't embarrassed.

' — ain't partial to the habit.'

He laughed again to show that he knew how ridiculous this was even though he wouldn't go so far as to be disloyal and say so. Carey shrugged, hooked a plug out of the leather pouch and settled it inside his cheek.

Glaze got up and peered over the ledge again. Miller had started to heap stones over Cobb's body.

4

As daylight bled away, Glaze and Sergeant Carey watched Miller build a cairn over Newt Cobb's body. He took time to consider his handiwork, walked round it and packed in more stones where he could. When he finished, they saw him turn his attention to the supplies. He made two parcels, bound them with twine and slung them over his shoulder.

Picking his way between the boulders which lined the edge of the river, Miller set out back along the valley floor to the place where he had climbed down. Once again, Glaze and Carey kept parallel with his progress on the trail high above.

As he walked along, Miller did not once look up. Glaze wanted some acknowledgement — as an officer, he expected it. He required some kind of signal to report on what Miller had found down there. Miller must have known Glaze was watching from the path. Glaze felt hot under his shirt; a line of sweat ran down his back even though the sun had not warmed the mountain air all day.

When they reached the ledge where Schmidt waited with the horses, all three of them leaned over the edge.

'Is he bringing supplies?' Schmidt's voice shook.

'He's done well.' Carey turned to Glaze. 'You got to admit that.'

Glaze didn't answer. Far below them, Miller started to climb.

The first few yards were easy; Miller could pick his way over the rocks without a hand hold. But the cliff side quickly became steep. He had to edge round boulders; there was loose scree underfoot and at times, the rock was sheer.

From above, the men could see the two packages slung from his shoulders; Miller had made lanyards and hung them round his neck. Each time he leaned out from the cliff to look for a handhold, the parcels swung and pulled him away from the rock face. More than once his boot slipped and he missed his footing, his hand failed to find a hold or a root he was hanging on to came away.

After a few yards' progress, Miller's holds seemed to collapse in his grip. Whether it was the weight of the packs pulling him off the cliff face, a lapse of concentration after so much effort or just a missed footing, Glaze and the others couldn't tell. As loose stones clattered around him, they watched him slide back down the rock to where he started.

Glaze felt his stomach turn. What if Miller didn't make it? So far the mission had yielded no results; they were three weeks out and had seen neither hide nor hair of the Crowleys. He had lost a man and all his supplies. Glaze was sweating inside his uniform again. Bolt's orders echoed in his head:

'Take a month's worth of supplies.' He could have objected; he could have said it was too late in the year. This mission was doomed from the start.

Miller's next attempt took an hour. Glaze and the others watched helplessly. They willed every grip to hold, every step to find firm ground. For a while it worked. He was halfway up before a buck brush root came away in his hand. The sudden shift in his weight caused the packs to swing and his foot to slip. It was worse this time. He tumbled over and over.

The packs flew out wide; their twine lanyards flung themselves round Miller's neck. He clutched at his throat to stop himself being strangled. With no free hand to steady himself against the rock face, momentum picked him up and hurled him downward, head over heels. His body twisted and bounced against the rock until it seemed that every muscle must be torn and every bone broken. Carey screamed Miller's name as if that might pull him back but the sound was swallowed by the roar of the water below. Glaze gripped the edge of the path until his knuckles cracked and the rock cut his hands.

Stumbling to his feet, Carey started to lower himself over the edge of the path. Glaze yelled something then. He grabbed Carey's jacket and hung on. He yelled for Schmidt to help him. The big man seized Carey by his shoulders and heaved him back.

'Stay up here,' Glaze screamed. 'That's an order.'

Schmidt dumped the sergeant in a heap.

All three of them hung over the edge and stared down to where Miller lay. None of them spoke. For a long time, Miller didn't move.

Dusk turned to darkness. Shadows gathered in the ravine below the three men. Night sat in the fissures of the cliff and painted the rocky slopes flat. It became impossible to tell where the edge of the river was, where water ended and solid ground began. The unending roar of the river played on the nerves of the men. Miller's body was heaped on the bank. Pretty soon the darkness would capture him, too.

'Let me go down there,' Carey said. 'He's hurt. Gotta be.'

'I'll go,' Schmidt said.

'You'll never be able to climb back up again,' Glaze snapped. 'You saw what just happened.'

'We can't leave our own,' Carey insisted.

Glaze turned up the collar of his jacket and dug his hands in his pockets. The temperature was falling.

'He was ordered not to go, Sergeant,' Glaze said.

'He went to help a fallen man.' Carey looked Glaze in the eye. 'He went to fetch provisions for all of us.'

Glaze looked away; his thoughts swerved. Carey thought he was wrong. He thought they should have climbed down when Cobb fell. Cobb would still have died but they would have had the provisions. Carey thought they could have carried the supplies between them and made their way by the river; they should be sitting down there around a fire with their bellies full right now.

It was still possible to make out the arch of Miller's body. He was curled in on himself with his back upwards, not spread-eagled like Cobb had been. Glaze stared hard through the remains of the light trying to detect some movement, some sign, however slight, that Miller was alive. There was nothing.

'We wait till morning,' Glaze said abruptly. 'No one could make it down there in this light.'

'Sir.' Carey's reply was automatic.

Ordinarily, Glaze would not have cared whether the sergeant agreed with an order or not; back at the fort, it wouldn't even have crossed his mind to wonder. But out here, after what had happened to Cobb, it mattered. Nightfall had bought Glaze the time to decide what to do.

Thoughts of the answers he might

give Bolt came into his head. He had ordered Miller not to go. He had informed the sergeant that Private Miller would be on a charge. No, he had not attempted to ascertain whether Cobb was alive. No, he had not attempted to recover the supplies. Inside his jacket pocket, he clenched his fist tight. Glaze stayed staring down at Miller's body until shadows buried it.

Carey and Schmidt sat together in the lee of the cliff and passed Carey's tobacco pouch between them.

'Anything?' Carey looked up at him.

'Nothing, Sergeant,' Glaze said. 'He ain't moved at all.'

Carey nudged Schmidt. 'Go and find us some kindling. Looks like we're here for the night.'

Glaze sat down beside them. The ground was hard and the rock he leaned against broke his back. He pulled his jacket tight against the cold, cupped his hands and blew into them to feel some warmth on his face.

'Ain't you got hard tack in your saddle-bag?' Carey said.

Schmidt was already by the horses.

'No,' Glaze said. 'Don't keep my own provisions.'

He felt the sergeant looking at him.

'I'll let you have some of mine,' Carey said.

It was too dark for Glaze to see the expression on his face.

'Half now,' Schmidt said with his mouth full, 'half when I get back.'

The big man strode off up the track.

'Might as well make a fire,' Carey said. 'Even if we ain't got nothing to cook on it.'

He broke off a piece of hard tack and handed it to Glaze.

'I'm grateful, Sergeant.'

It was a generous gesture.

'Never keep a piece of hard tack by for emergencies?' Carey said.

'All provisions and foodstuffs should be kept and issued by the NCO designate at the appropriate times,' Glaze quoted from regulations.

'I ignore all that,' Carey said. 'I tell the men to keep a piece in their saddle-bags.' He laughed. 'They appreciate it.'

It was cold now. Glaze pulled the collar of his jacket up round his throat and hugged his arms round himself. He had never heard anyone confess so openly to an infringement of army rules. Carey was stoical, loyal and trustworthy; Glaze knew that. To discover he had cut across regulations in the first place was a surprise but to find he encouraged the men to do the same and then admitted to it took Glaze's words away. The hard tack was dry and salty in his mouth and tasted as glorious as peaches on a summer afternoon.

Why had Carey told him? He had made a point of it, hadn't he? He could have made out it was a mistake. He could have said nothing. Glaze felt hot again under his shirt. Was Carey offering him some kind of challenge? Did he want his lieutenant to start defending a regulation that had served them so badly?

'Thanks,' Glaze said.

He felt sweat prick his neck where he had turned up his collar against the cold. Right now it was better to say nothing, better to make out he hadn't noticed. He couldn't afford for Carey to take against him, not out here. That would jeopardize the success of the mission. He would just keep an eye on his sergeant; he would keep alert to any signs he might undermine him — his tone of voice, any throwaway remarks.

Glaze leaned back against the rock, took a swig from his canteen and stared out into the darkness. The water was so cold it seared his throat. He could offer his canteen to Carey. That would show he had no hard feelings; it would repay him for the hard tack.

'Got enough water?' Glaze said.

He held out his canteen.

'Thanks,' Carey said. 'Mine's full.'

Again Glaze felt sweat prick under his collar, just a small discomfort. He took another swallow of water and screwed back the cap.

'How far is it to the cairn?' Carey said.

'Day's ride or thereabouts,' Glaze said.

'Will we make it by tomorrow night?' Carey's voice was anxious.

Why was Carey pressing him? Glaze had already given him an answer.

'You've been up there?' Carey went on. 'You've seen it?'

Did he doubt him now? Glaze felt the edge of his collar against his neck.

'Colonel Bolt issued instructions to the first train that passed through the fort last spring,' Glaze explained. 'Told them to build it and to leave whatever provisions they could underneath. Next train to come through would use the supplies and leave something in exchange. That way there would always be something there if a storm blew in or a wagon got stranded up there.'

'You've seen it yourself?' Carey insisted. 'It's one thing for the colonel to issue an order to a wagon train that's passing through . . . '

Glaze heard uncertainty in the sergeant's voice, the need to be assured that the colonel's system worked. Didn't he trust what Glaze was telling him?

'Rode up there with the second train,' Glaze said. 'Cairn was right where the colonel said it would be. Men from the train uncovered the supplies and left fresh in exchange.'

He looked over at Carey. The sergeant was leaning his head back against the rock wall, staring out into the night. Darkness filled the ravine now; Glaze could barely make out the sergeant's face.

'How many trains been through since then?' Carey said.

They heard footsteps further along the track. Carey jumped to his feet. 'Schmidt, that you?'

'Me, Sarge.'

The footsteps got louder. A few loose stones clattered over the edge of the ravine. Then Schmidt was beside them, out of breath through hurrying, a bundle of kindling in his arms.

'Black as pitch out there,' Schmidt said. 'Getting colder, too.'

He dropped the sticks where he stood.

'I'm gonna have the other half of that hard tack before I light the fire.' Schmidt hesitated. 'You saving the tallow?'

'What?' Carey sounded puzzled.

'The candle,' Schmidt laughed. 'Come on, Sarge.'

'What candle? What are you talking about?'

'Don't leave me standing here in the dark, Sarge. Just light the candle so I can find my hard tack. Then I'll make the fire.'

'What are you talking about?'

'The candle lantern.' Schmidt was tired, at the end of his patience. 'I know you've got one. We've been out three weeks and I've never seen it. Did you just come across it in a saddle-bag?'

'The type the wagons use?' Carey said. 'Never carry one of those.'

'Is it you, Lieutenant?' Schmidt was addressing Glaze. 'Sarge is ribbing me. Would you light the lantern?'

'There ain't no lantern,' Carey snapped. 'Find your hard tack in the dark, just like we did.'

Schmidt was silent. The others heard him going through the contents of his saddle-bag. Then he said firmly, 'I saw a lantern when I was a ways up the track. I looked back and there it was. Must have been close to where we are now.'

Carey sat down. Glaze heard him feel in his jacket for his tobacco.

'You're sure?' Glaze said.

'Yes, Lieutenant,' Schmidt said. There was hard tack in his mouth. 'That's why I thought Sarge was ribbing me. It was close to where we are now. A few yards back down the path, maybe. Then it went out. I thought Sarge was saving on the tallow.'

Glaze levered himself to his feet and stepped out from the rock wall. The night made him blind. It was too dark even to see the edge of the path; he couldn't tell whether the others stood close beside him or were yards away. He stared up and down where he imagined the path was. He saw blackness and heard the roar of water boom in his ears. Away from the shelter of the cliff side, the night wind stung his face.

After a while, being surrounded by darkness made Glaze unsteady on his feet. He turned back to the shelter of the cliff side. Schmidt struck his flint to try to make a fire but the handful of onion grass he had brought back as kindling was damp.

'Couldn't see nothing,' Glaze said.

Carey struggled to take shavings from the one dry stick he found in Schmidt's bundle. Eventually, he coaxed a flame. The damp wood made a meagre fire but the men sat close and held their palms out flat.

After an hour, the wind picked up. Its

moan echoed the length of the ravine. They had heard the wind sound like this on other nights and it had never bothered them. But tonight, without Cobb and Miller, the sound preyed on their nerves. It reminded them of how alone they were and how exposed. The things they usually relied on to get them through — their courage, their comrades and their army discipline — seemed frail and barely adequate. Their strength was diminished by the cold and eroded by the ghostly whine of the wind.

The fire died. The men curled themselves up, trying to have as little of their bodies in contact with the freezing rock as they could, and lay still. Carey fished in his tobacco pouch.

'I did see something,' Schmidt said suddenly. 'Believe me, don't you, Sarge? I reckon there's someone out there.'

The men sat upright and strained their eyes into the darkness until imaginary patterns dazzled them. Their hearts raced and crashed under their ribs. Glaze's army issue Colt was cold in his hand.

'You're seeing things, Schmidt,' Carey said. 'Just try and get some sleep.'

5

Sleep came in snatches of minutes at a time. When the men were awake, their senses were deprived. The roar of water deafened their ears; the darkness blinded them; the cold stole smell from the air. Where their legs were drawn up under them or their arms were cradled under their heads, their limbs froze into numbness. Cold slipped out of the rock and into their bones to stiffen their joints and harden their muscles until the smallest movement was agony.

Glaze slept curled up on his side with his hands tucked inside his jacket so his fingertips rested on the letter in his inside pocket. He tried to conjure images of warmth, nights spent out on the trail beside a blazing fire or sitting by some hearth watching the flames rear. But these pictures would not stay. The pain of the cold gripping his muscles and biting his joints knocked them out of his head and made him concentrate on hard rock, scouring air and empty darkness.

Schmidt spent most of the night standing between the horses. When he had extracted warmth from their bodies, or when standing became too much he would come and lie down again. Carey curled himself up and snored.

As night weakened in the east, tiny snowflakes filled the air and settled on the rock around the men. Glaze opened his eyes to the sound of something scrabbling on the cliff nearby. Disorientated, aching with cold and with hunger stabbing his belly, he assumed some animal had picked up their scent. Schmidt was standing by the horses again; Carey was struggling to sit up. They had all heard it.

Glaze reached for his gun. Schmidt's story about seeing a lantern came into his head. They heard loose stones skitter down the side of the cliff. Then

Miller's head popped up over the lip of the path; his hat was dusted with snow.

Carey leapt over towards him, grabbed his arm and heaved him on to the path. Schmidt finished lacing the saddle-bags and joined him.

'Boy, it's good to see you.' Carey was jubilant.

He hauled Miller to his feet, threw his arms round his shoulders and hugged him close.

'Thought you'd have a fire up here,' Miller said. He collapsed in a heap on the hard ground, winded and laughing with relief.

He looked at the pile of wet sticks they had tried to light.

'I brought breakfast.'

He fished a linen bag of coffee out of one pocket and a hunk of raw bacon the size of a dinner plate out of the other.

'We got some hard tack in the saddle-bags,' Carey said. This'll do us fine for now.' He turned to Glaze. 'Looks like we'll be relying on the supplies under that cairn.'

'Brung all I could carry,' Miller said. He was bursting with pride at having made it back. 'Weight I had on me yesterday pulled me off the cliff.'

'You climbed all the way up in the dark?' Glaze said.

'Too cold down there by the water.' Miller sat back, exhausted. 'Ain't so hard if you don't carry much.'

Glaze had it in mind to tell Miller he was on a charge. He had disobeyed a direct order. Miller would expect it. As the officer present, it was Glaze's duty. But Carey's genuine delight in seeing the man and Miller's good spirits stopped him from speaking out. He would wait. After a hard night, morale was picking up; he should encourage that.

'There's a cave right below here,' Miller said. 'Dry wood in there. Just climbed past it.'

'I'll go,' Carey said quickly. 'Schmidt can wait on the edge and haul me up.' He looped his hands in a line of rope and threw the end to Schmidt.

Glaze watched the men. Carey should have checked with him first but he didn't. He knew Glaze forbade Miller from going down the cliff side yesterday but he still went ahead. Miller had probably forgotten but it rankled. Little by little, Glaze felt his authority being chipped away.

Carey lowered himself over the lip of the path. His peg leg stuck out like a minute hand. Schmidt coiled the rope round his waist ready to haul him back. Miller sat down gratefully and leaned back against the wall of the cliff. Grey morning light filled the sky and a shower of tiny snowflakes blew in on a cold east wind.

'Could tell him now,' Glaze thought. Then it would be out in the open. Officer and enlisted man would know where they stood. In spite of the cold, Glaze felt hot again; his collar chafed his neck.

Miller had leaned his head back against the rock and closed his eyes to snatch a moment's rest. He must have felt Glaze staring at him, though, as he opened them again almost immediately.

'Got a pocket full of oats for the horses,' Miller said. 'That was all I could carry.'

He hadn't said, 'Lieutenant'. Glaze curled his fingers into the palm of his hand.

Carey shouted from somewhere below. A second later he started to pass dry sticks up to Schmidt, who threw them behind him on to the ledge. After a while, Carey called out again. Schmidt leaned down and hauled Carey back.

'Been on top of that all night and never knew it was there,' Carey said. He was pleased with himself.

'He's brought oats for the horses,' Glaze said.

'With respect, sir,' Carey hesitated. 'The horses ain't eaten since yesterday but neither have we. Shouldn't we be saving everything for ourselves?'

'No.'

The sharpness in Glaze's voice made the men look up.

'I mean, you know we've got to feed the horses,' Glaze said. He had it on the tip of his tongue to quote from the manual but bit back his words.

Snow was falling quickly, a wall of tiny flakes.

'I only meant that a few oats between four horses ain't going to make much difference, sir.' Carey pressed his point. 'It would be a meal to us.'

'Feed the horses, Sergeant.' Glaze's smile was a disguise. 'We look after them, they look after us.'

Carey nodded to Schmidt, who took the oats from Miller and held them in cupped hands to each of the horses in turn. Carey got a fire going. No one remarked on the snow.

As soon as the flames bit on the dry wood, the men moved in close. Carey steadied the blaze with some of the previous night's wet kindling. The fire hissed; smoke caught under the over-hanging rock. Carey stabbed the lump

69

of bacon with his knife and held it over the flames.

'Get your cups,' Carey said.

'Ain't got no coffee pot, Sarge,' Schmidt said.

'In my saddle-bag,' Carey said.

Carey caught Glaze's eye. Same as the hard tack, Glaze thought. Regulations required each man to carry his own plate-cup and fork. Foodstuffs, supplies and perishable goods along with all cooking equipment were to be carried by the quartermaster or trooper in charge of supplies.

The smell of bacon hung in the air. As Carey turned his knife, fat dripped through the flames and burst in little explosions on the burning wood. Schmidt passed round the coffee pot. Without being asked, each man added a measure of water from his canteen. They couldn't take their eyes off the bacon.

'Bacon sure smells good.' Schmidt was genuinely excited at the thought of food. He clapped a huge arm round

Miller's shoulder. 'And you knew where there was firewood to cook it on.'

Carey laughed and turned the bacon again. The outside was blackened now; fat ran out in a steady stream now, and hissed and popped in the flames. The smell was mouthwatering. Glaze loosened his collar and held his hands flat against the heat from the fire.

Right in front of their eyes, in teasing slow motion, the lump of meat separated down both sides of Carey's knife and plopped into the pile of burning sticks. Pandemonium. The men shouted and grabbed for it. Miller got there first and managed to snatch one lump and flick it, plastered with twigs and charcoal, out of the fire on to the rock floor. Schmidt got the other. In the process of the four of them making a dive for the food, the coffee pot up-ended, doused the fire and a cloud of steam exploded in their faces.

Everyone yelled. Carey made a stab for the piece of bacon nearest him; Schmidt blew on his hands; Miller flipped the hunk of bacon on to a tin plate. When Glaze righted the coffee pot, there was half a cup left. The fire, meagre enough to begin with, was out.

The men stopped shouting as quickly as they started. They took stock of their breakfast. Miller scraped the ash off the bacon and divided it into equal shares. Glaze poured the coffee into a tin cup.

'There's only enough for a mouthful each,' Glaze said.

'Let Miller have it,' Carey said.

Glaze caught his eye. He had been just about to suggest the same thing; Carey had got there first. Carey could have asked him, Glaze thought. Back at the fort he would have.

'Nice of you, Sarge,' Miller said. 'But it was my fault the coffee got spilt.'

'It was an accident,' Carey smiled at him.

Glaze had to say something or Carey would be in charge of the whole shebang.

'You brought it all the way up here,' he said.

The men turned towards him as though his words puzzled them. Glaze felt heat rise in his face.

'Least we got hard tack to have with it,' Miller said. He forced cheerfulness into his voice. 'Bacon and hard tack — almost like being back at the fort.'

'Ate the hard tack last night,' Carey said. 'All we had against the cold.'

Glaze thought he saw Carey glance at him but he couldn't tell.

'Not me,' Miller crowed. 'I was lying down there thinking all my bones was broke. I'm about to make up for it right now.'

Miller left his plate beside the fire and pushed himself to his feet. The others helped themselves to their share of the bacon. They ate slowly; the hot, salty meat was beyond luxury; the warm grease was nectar in their throats.

Schmidt ate with his eyes closed. The big man sat there, head back, blissful smile on his face, the plate of a few scraps of bacon balanced in his huge hands. Carey grinned at this; he had

73

seen him do it before. He nudged Glaze to invite him in on the joke.

'Hey.' There was a sudden shout from over by the horses. 'Someone's been in my saddle-bag.'

Miller held open the flaps of his saddle-bag with one hand and rummaged through the contents with the other. He pulled the saddle-bag off the horse, brought it over to where they were sitting and flung it on the ground.

'See that?' he demanded.

Miller's face was red. His shoulders dropped and his hands clenched into fists.

He glared at each of them in turn.

'Who did it?'

Glaze and the others stopped chewing. Glaze was shocked to be spoken to like this by one of the men.

'Did what?' Carey said.

'Ate my hard tack, that's what.'

Miller's voice was like a whiplash.

They all knew. Carey turned to Schmidt.

'You were over by the horses half the

night,' Carey said coldly. 'Must have been you.'

Schmidt crammed the last of his bacon into his mouth and chewed fast. He looked wildly from one to the other of them.

'Might have known,' Miller roared. 'You've always been a greedy — '

Miller launched himself at Schmidt. He slung a right; his fist cracked against the big man's cheekbone. Schmidt yelled and struggled to shove himself to his feet, but Miller was on top of him, battering him with wild punches. As Schmidt kicked out, the remains of the smoldering sticks from the fire scattered everywhere. Glaze jumped back; Carey grabbed Miller round the throat and heaved him off. Miller's last punch arced through the empty air.

'Enough,' Carey roared.

He wrenched Miller back on top of him, his forearm locked across Miller's throat. Half strangled, exploding with fury, Miller tore at Carey's arm; his face blackened as his air supply was cut.

'If I let you go, are you gonna lay off?' Carey yelled.

He clamped his arm tighter round Miller's throat. Miller nodded desperately; a throttled cry escaped from his throat. Carey jerked his grip again.

'You sure?'

Miller waved his hands wildly. Carey gave one last heave at Miller's neck and shoved him aside. Miller lay doubled over, racked by coughing, jagged breaths shredding his lungs. His hands protectively clutched his throat.

Carey heaved himself from underneath Miller's body and levered himself to his feet. He rounded on Schmidt.

'I should throw you off this cliff right now,' he bellowed. 'All the supplies is down there. Old Newt ain't gonna be eating any; you could have 'em all to yourself.'

Schmidt cowered. He raised his hands over his face.

'Maybe I will,' Carey ranted. 'Maybe I will throw you off. Ain't no one here gonna say they saw nothin'.'

'Sarge, please,' Schmidt implored him.

He kept his guard up in case Carey lunged at him.

'We all saw him fall down there. He wasn't moving. The lieutenant said we wasn't to go down after him.' Schmidt pleaded for pity.

'So what?' Carey snarled. 'Did me or the lieutenant go through his saddle-bags? Was we the ones who ate his tack?'

'I thought Miller was dead, Sarge.' Schmidt's voice fell to a whisper. 'I thought he's got to be dead otherwise the lieutenant would order you or me to go down after him. The lieutenant wouldn't leave none of us down there if we was alive.'

'Well, he ain't dead.' Carey hesitated. 'You didn't have no proof he was. Anyhow, it still didn't give you the right to steal nothing.'

'Private Schmidt, I'm placing you on a charge.' Glaze's words cut across them. His voice was steel. 'You'll be dealt with when we get back to the fort.'

Schmidt lowered his hands and looked up at the officer.

'Sir.'

Miller still writhed on the ground; each breath clawed at his throat.

'And you, Miller,' Glaze went on. 'You're on a charge for breaches of discipline. I ain't letting none of this pass.'

Glaze nodded to Carey.

'Do what you have to, Sergeant.'

'Sir.' Surprise crossed Carey's face. 'Out here, do you think . . . ?'

'I have placed these men on a charge, Sergeant.' Glaze's words were clear and precise. 'All men on a charge are required to surrender their weapons.'

Carey hesitated again.

'Those are the regulations,' Glaze stated, as if explanation were needed. 'You know it just as well as I.'

Carey nudged Schmidt with the toe of his boot and nodded towards his gun. Schmidt unbuttoned the flap of his

holster and handed over his army issue
Colt. Carey knelt down beside Miller
and took the pistol from his belt. He
offered the weapons to Glaze.

'Thank you, Sergeant. The weapons
will remain in my charge for the
remainder of the mission.'

Glaze emptied the chambers of both
Colts into his hand. He strode over to
his horse, placed both weapons together
with the ammunition in his own
saddle-bag and tied the laces firmly.

The snow fell like a wall. The
opposite side of the ravine had
disappeared. It was impossible to see
more than a couple of yards either way
along the track. The overhang where
the men sheltered was filled with cold
grey light.

Glaze sat down against a wall
opposite Carey and the men. For a
while he watched the bright falling
snow but eventually his vision blurred
and he felt dizzy. He stared at the
ground to avoid looking into the faces
of the men. He had done well, he

thought. He had secured his authority. The private soldiers were on a charge and that had brought an end to the brawling. He pulled his jacket round him.

'We'll wait here until the weather lifts,' he said.

6

The whiteout continued all morning.

Carey organized tasks for the men, which kept them apart. Miller rebuilt the fire and struggled to light it; Schmidt brushed the horses. They got on with things in a sullen, routine way much as they would back at the fort. Glaze made a show of keeping an eye on their work.

As Miller struggled with his flint, Glaze said, 'See anything when you were down there last night?'

'Lieutenant?'

Miller looked up; it was the kind of question officers asked when they hadn't really grasped what was going on. It always surprised him, though he had seen enough of officers to know that it shouldn't; if one of the enlisted men had asked a question like that, he would have laughed. Miller could see by the look on Glaze's face that he genuinely wanted to know. He forced himself not to smile.

'Any lights?' Glaze said. 'Any sign of anyone down there? Anything at all?'

Lights. That was a clue, Miller thought. Talking to officers was like deciphering a code. You had to work out what they meant.

'Black as pitch, Lieutenant,' Miller said. 'Nearly slipped into the river a couple of times.'

'No sign of anyone?' Glaze repeated.

Why couldn't he just come out with it? Miller thought. He was driving at something. Why couldn't he just say what it was? Miller's throat felt as if he had swallowed glass; the sarge had practically torn out his windpipe. He was starving hungry and cold to the bone, to say nothing of the fact that he had inched his way up the cliff in the dark. Now, here was this officer hinting at something and not saying what it was. Miller turned back to the fire.

'Nothing at all?' Glaze said.

What did he want him to say? Miller scraped his flint but the wood was wet and there was nothing to use as kindling.

'When Schmidt went out, he saw a light,' Glaze said.

There it was. Miller sparked his flint again. That greedy fool had seen something. Now the lieutenant was asking him if he had seen it, too. Maybe it wasn't all officers, Miller reflected, maybe it was just this one.

'Like I said, it was black as pitch, Lieutenant,' Miller repeated. 'Only light was your lantern up here — '

'What?' Glaze interrupted him. 'You saw it?'

Miller stared at him. No, not all officers were like this.

'Your lantern,' Miller went on cautiously. 'Made me wish I was up here, I can tell you.'

Glaze continued to stare at him.

'Thought you must be searching for firewood,' Miller said. 'Waited to see the flames.'

At midday the snow eased. A driving wall of small flakes had angled past the overhang since first light; now the flakes were as wide as feathers and drifted down lazily. Sunlight broke through and the falling snow sparkled. From where the men sheltered, they could make out the outline of the opposite side of the ravine.

Glaze and Sergeant Carey ducked out from under the overhang to inspect the path. Snow lay six inches deep. The path was wide here, but higher up, it narrowed sharply. There were two questions. One: was there ice under the snow? Two: could the horses make it? The men walked a few yards up the path and kicked away the surface snow while the falling flakes decorated their hats and shoulders.

'Lose a horse up here, it's a long walk home,' Miller said. 'Newt Cobb fell even before there was any snow.'

'Don't talk about him.' Glaze was clearly irritated. 'That's in the past.'

Questions Colonel Bolt might want

answered were still on his mind; he didn't have answers to all of them. He loosened the collar of his shirt.

The two men walked on, scraping the snow away after almost every step. After a few yards, they both knew that it was too dangerous for the horses. The powdery snow disguised a film of ice over the path; the first fall had frozen hard during the early hours.

'Could lead the horses,' Carey suggested. 'Don't have to ride 'em.'

Glaze walked ahead; he stared down at the track and kicked snow aside as he went.

'Can't go back this way,' Carey went on helpfully. 'Cobb took that piece of the track with him.'

Glaze turned on him.

'We got no food. It's a day's ride to the cairn, maybe more. I've lost a man and will have to answer questions for it.'

Snowflakes fell between them like a screen.

'Might be able to go quicker on foot,' Carey suggested. 'If we left the horses here, at least they'd rest up.'

'We'll have to take the wagon trail back down,' Glaze snapped. 'How long will that take on foot?'

'If the weather eases,' Carey suggested, 'one of us could come back for the horses.'

The men stared out across the valley. Carey watched the flakes, which twinkled like diamonds in the sunshine. Glaze felt shut in; the sun through the falling snow was like daylight through prison bars.

'Another thing,' Glaze said. 'We ain't alone out here.'

Carey stopped in his tracks.

'Miller saw the light from down in the valley. Thought it was a candle lantern. Schmidt saw the same thing.'

Carey hesitated. With the bright sunlight reflecting off the snow crystals, the pure snow heaped along the path and the clean mountain air in his lungs, such a thing seemed impossible.

'He said so?' Carey said.

'He thought one of us was out

looking for firewood,' Glaze snapped.

Carey looked around him at the snow, the mountainside and at their own footprints behind them along the path. It was impossible.

'We ain't seen no tracks,' he said.

Glaze waved away Carey's response. He turned abruptly and strode back down the path making sure he jabbed his boot heels into the ice. Carey scuttled after him and caught up with him outside the overhang.

'Lieutenant,' Carey was breathless. 'Reckon it's the Crowleys?'

'I believe, Sergeant,' Glaze said deliberately, 'that we must have good order, obedience and military discipline. That way we can get up to the cairn and renew our supplies.'

Glaze ducked under the overhang. Miller was helping Schmidt brush the horses. The men looked up quickly as if they had been interrupted sharing some private conversation. He felt the eyes of the men watching him but he avoided their gaze. He busied himself by taking off his hat, knocking the snow onto the rock floor and brushing off his shoulders. His saddle-bag, which contained Schmidt's and Miller's Colts, was untouched where he had left it.

'No fire?' Glaze looked over at Miller.

At his feet was a heap of blackened sticks. The coffee pot stood beside it.

'Wood's too wet, Lieutenant,' Miller said. 'Even when I shaved some down, it wouldn't take a spark.'

Glaze sat down against a rock wall. He had expected a fire. Schmidt and Miller turned back to the horses. They weren't looking at him. Had they turned away suddenly when he came back in? It was agony being trapped here all together. On exercise on the plains or even back at the fort, there was always some place you could go to make space for yourself. Forced into closeness like this, you felt you couldn't breathe.

Carey brushed the snow off his coat.

'Those horses have never been so well looked after,' he called brightly.

The men grinned at him.

Glaze stared out into the snow. At least it was warmer than last night. Carey went over to join the men. He took time inspecting their work; he commented on it and told them how well they'd done. Glaze heard him move the conversation into a discussion about the horses; Carey asked their opinions and soon they sounded like dealers at an auction.

After a while, Glaze stopped trying to overhear. He stared into the snow until it made patterns in front of his eyes. For a moment he forgot where he was. He stretched out his legs in front of him. The sound of the men's voices died away. Fatigue from the broken night, the ache of hunger and the wearying cold in his bones all disappeared. He was on the edge of sleep.

Glaze's hand slipped inside his jacket and touched the edge of the letter tucked in the pocket. Colonel Bolt's words echoed in his head: 'All the reason I need to bump you up to captain again.' When his name rang out across the parade ground, Glaze stood tall, shoulders back, and pride swelled his chest until he thought he would burst. Colonel Bolt could have picked anyone, but he picked him. He wanted them all to hear his name, officers and men. Bolt was giving him a second chance. He had faith in him. Even after what had happened, he was the one who was chosen. Bolt never gave second chances, but this time he had.

'Lieutenant?'

Glaze came out of his reverie smiling. The three of them were standing there looking down at him. Anxious, unhappy faces. Glaze was suddenly aware of the cold in his limbs. His joints were so stiff he could hardly move.

'Lieutenant?'

Carey leaned over to help him up; Glaze waved him away. He pushed against the rock wall and levered himself to his feet.

'We were wondering if you'd decided about the horses?'

We. What did Carey mean, we? What was he talking about? Then Glaze realized it had stopped snowing. Outside the overhang, light flooded the valley. Not the intense bright sunshine that made the falling snow sparkle and promised to warm the air; this light was threadbare as if the day had already worn itself out.

'We leave them,' Glaze said quickly. 'Proceed on foot to the cairn. If the snow thaws, we come back and get them. If it doesn't we take the wagon trail back to the fort. Either way, we'll have supplies.'

'What about the mission, sir?' Carey looked anxious.

Glaze felt hot suddenly as if he was feverish. He had told them what they were going to do. He had made the decision and given clear and straightforward orders. Now Carey wanted more explanation. How much more could he give? Glaze heard Bolt's clipped, military voice: 'If this is successful, I'll have all the reason I need.'

'We'll keep lookout,' Glaze said. 'One step at a time, Sergeant. The priority right now is to get up to the cairn where the supplies are.'

That pleased them. He had done well, Glaze thought. He saw the way their shoulders dropped and they relaxed when he told them they would all be going. They knew there was a risk in leaving the horses unguarded and they knew he had considered it and come to a decision. More than that, where some officers might have decided to leave a man behind to stand guard over military property, he had not. The men could see that Lieutenant Glaze had put them first.

'Want me to take point again?' Miller said.

There. Miller had volunteered. That would influence Schmidt; Sergeant Carey would hear it.

'Sir, request permission to carry my weapon while on point duty.'

Miller came smartly to attention. His face was a mask.

Glaze hesitated. Was that why Miller volunteered? Was this an attempt to put one over on him? He felt a drop of sweat prick the back of his neck. All three of them were watching him. He had won their trust and now he was about to lose it.

Either way it didn't add up, Glaze thought. If he gave Miller his gun he would be seen to have backed down; if he didn't they would think he had put a man in harm's way.

'Every man will carry out point duties in rotation.' Glaze's words were abrupt and formal. 'I'll take the first turn.'

He paused and looked out at the thin sunlight. The wall of rock on the opposite side of the ravine was clear now.

'Privates Schmidt and Miller will follow me. Sergeant Carey will bring up the rear. Sergeant Carey will also carry the saddle-bag containing the weapons of the men on a charge.'

He saw Miller staring at him. He felt

needle pricks at the back of his neck again. Miller was insolent; it was in his blood.

Glaze set a good pace even though the track was steep. His breath formed a cloud in front of his face. The temperature had fallen and there was a thin crust of ice on the snow. The weak sun struggled through the clouds but did not warm the air.

The snow crunched under Glaze's boots. Behind him, he could hear Schmidt and Miller chat good naturedly as they walked along. He couldn't make out what they were saying and he didn't turn round. That should be Carey and himself. He would have appreciated the sergeant's company. Instead, he was out in front and Carey was carrying the men's weapons yards behind. Maybe he should just have given Miller his Colt and let him walk ahead as he had wanted. The back of his neck burned.

The trail narrowed to not much more than a goat path. They would have struggled to bring the horses along here even without lying snow. The drop was sheer on the left side; the cliff fell away hundreds of feet. Soon they had climbed so far that the white water below them was almost inaudible. The ravine widened out; the opposite side was scarred by deep clefts left by avalanches and wide flat surfaces where tons of rock had broken away at the fault lines and slid into the valley below.

Glaze felt stones underfoot. For the moment they were held by the layer of ice, but when a thaw came they would be loose and treacherous.

Colonel Bolt had suggested this route; he said he had ridden it himself. Difficult enough for horses, there was no chance of getting a wagon up here. Did Bolt know that? Was that why he had picked Glaze over the other officers, because it was difficult?

Then another thought came to him, one which was not welcome. The effort of the climb suddenly made him sweat under his clothes. Had Bolt already asked the others and they had refused?

Had they said it was too late in the year? Had they said their men were used to the plains, not the mountains?

The plains. Had Bolt asked him because of what had happened out there? Did he still blame him for that? Was that why he had chosen him to lead this mission? Glaze kicked the snow aside and dug his boot heels into the ice.

They climbed into cloud. Or the cloud was lowering itself on to them. Thick mist surrounded them. Glaze couldn't see the way ahead; the valley was gone and he could barely make out the edge of the path. He looked back; the men were trudging after him, heads bowed. Schmidt and Miller had stopped talking.

'Lieutenant,' Carey called. He dug his wooden leg into the ice. 'Suggest we rest up a while.' He sounded out of breath.

'No,' Glaze shouted. 'We keep going.'

7

An hour later, Miller was on point. As the men climbed, low cloud buried them until they could barely see a foot ahead. There was no day or night, just bleached grey light without a hint of where the sun might be. It disorientated them. The mist was as oppressive as a prison wall and as insubstantial as the air that held it. The edge of the path was invisible; to keep themselves from falling, they walked with one hand trailing along the wall of rock. A false step would tip them to their deaths.

The climb burned the muscles in their legs; the sharp air scraped their lungs; hunger pecked at their guts. No one spoke. At first, each of them sank into his own thoughts but as time went on, the effort of heaving one step after another numbed the power to think. They had no imaginings left; their minds were as empty as the mist that surrounded them. They forced themselves on, morose and exhausted.

Quite suddenly, they came through the cloud. It was a miracle. The sun burned like gold against a silk sky; snowy peaks stretched for miles in all directions and glittered like treasure. The path snaked ahead of them up the side of the cliff. Away to their left, a great open range of cloud stretched between the mountain tops and shone brilliant white in the sunshine. The men caught their breath, leaned against the rock wall and stared in awe.

It took a few minutes before any of them realized they were being watched. Further up the path, a wizened figure in deerskin clothes and wearing the head of a deer as a hat covered them with a Sharps hunting rifle. Glaze raised his hand in salute but the figure didn't move; the rifle stayed levelled at them.

'Coming up,' Glaze called.

He pushed ahead of Miller and walked slowly, keeping his hands away from his sides, palms open. The other men followed.

'Stop right there.'

The voice trilled like a bird but it was impossible to tell who the person was. The hat was the head of a buck with the crown of antlers still in place. The face, which peeped from under it, was burnished and creased like old leather; dark, darting eyes were screwed up against the sun. Bony hands stuck like claws out of the deerskin sleeves and gripped the rifle. The clumsily made deerskin suit disguised the small frame of the wearer. The men stared; the figure with the rifle stared back.

'Lost our supplies,' Glaze began. 'Sure like to trade some food.'

The figure looked from one to the other of them. The heavy rifle remained pointed at Glaze's chest, steady as a rock.

'Which one of you's my husband?'

The rifle barrel swung to Schmidt. 'Is it you, big fella?'

Schmidt backed into the rock.

'No. It ain't me.'

The currant eyes glittered under the deer head.

'I still got the rifle,' the voice screeched.

Glaze took a pace forward. 'None of us is your husband. I can assure you of that.'

The rifle barrel waved dangerously. The deer seemed unconvinced.

'Maybe we could help you look for him if you gave us some food,' Glaze suggested casually.

The deer head gave a wild screech. Although the men understood it was meant as laughter, it sounded more like the cry of a bird.

'Look for him? What for?'

The deer head turned and examined each of them in turn.

'You're looking for him, ain't you?' Glaze said carefully.

The deer head screeched again.

'I know where he is. He's inside.'

The rifle barrel waved towards a split in the rock.

Glaze was at a loss.

'Sure none of you ain't him?' The currant eyes burned under the deer head and checked each of them again.

'Ma'am,' Glaze said. 'I give you my word.'

'Ma'am?' the deer screeched. 'There ain't no ma'ams here.' The rifle barrel jabbed dangerously at Glaze. 'Who are you, anyways?'

'Look at us.' Carey spoke up. 'You can see none of us is your husband.'

The deer turned towards him.

'You make sense.' The Sharps waved at Glaze. 'This other one don't.'

'We're a mite confused,' Carey went on gently. 'You asked if one of us was your husband and then you said he was inside.'

'Ask him to come out,' Glaze interrupted. 'I'd like to speak to him.'

'You're a fool.' The deer looked to Carey for agreement. 'He's a fool, ain't he?'

In the middle of all this, Glaze knew the others were laughing at him.

Schmidt and Miller would be fighting to stay straight-faced; they would retell this story to each other later when he was out of earshot. They wouldn't mention that the Sharps was aimed at his chest all along.

'We're confused,' Carey said. 'That's all it is.'

The deer snorted. 'I know what a fool is and I think he is one.'

The great antlers swept backwards, as the buck raised its head to prove a point.

'Otherwise he wouldn't want my husband to come out and talk to him. How can he? My husband's dead.'

The antlers indicated the fissure in the rock, which the men now realized was the entrance to a cave.

'Dead?' Carey stared at the antlers, the deer head, the rifle.

'In there,' the deer said.

The deer watched Carey. 'Thought you were ghosts coming up out of the mist like that. My husband's ghost comes up that path sometimes when he's got something to say. Thought one of you was him come to see me again.'

'We ain't ghosts,' Glaze said. 'I can assure you of that.'

The deer looked at Carey.

'The fool's talking. 'Course I know you ain't ghosts. Had that figured a while back.'

'We'd like to trade some food,' Glaze pressed on.

'What have you got that I could possibly want?' the deer said.

'Ammunition?' Glaze suggested. 'Could let you have — '

'Got shells for a Sharps?'

'No,' Glaze admitted. He stared out across the bank of cloud, wishing the others hadn't heard.

'Could you let us have a little food?' Carey said.

'I could do that,' the deer said. 'My husband would like that. Ain't you got no food at all?'

'Nothing,' Carey said. 'Lost our wagon over the side.'

'How far back?' the deer said quickly.

103

'A day's walk.'

'All your supplies down there?'

'Right by the river,' Carey said. 'One of us went down but it was too steep to bring anything back up.'

'That right?' The deer seemed unconvinced. 'Which one went down there?'

'That'd be me,' Miller said.

'See any ghosts while you was down there by the white water?'

'Didn't see any,' Miller said carefully.

'Big fella with a beard,' the deer said. 'Plainsman's hat.'

'Sorry,' Miller said.

'Don't matter,' the deer said sadly. 'He was probably off somewhere. Half the time I don't know where he goes.'

'Mind telling us your name?' Carey said. 'Mine's Ben Carey.'

'Ain't got a name no more,' the deer said. 'Did have my husband's name, but since he's dead, ain't no point in me holding on to it. I had one before that but that was so long ago, it don't matter now. Anyhow, I was someone else back then.'

The deer pulled itself together. 'My husband left me this Sharps rifle when he died. That was a fine bequest, I reckon.'

'Sure was,' Carey said solemnly. The others nodded in agreement.

'Well, if one of you can make a fire, I can let you have something to cook on it.'

The deer angled itself sideways to squeeze through the fissure in the rock and a minute later emerged without the rifle, holding an armful of kindling.

Schmidt stepped forward.

'I'll make the fire.'

The deer eyed him for a moment as if it wasn't sure if he was up to the task, then came to a decision and dropped the wood in front of him. The others sat down and leaned back gratefully against the rock. The sun turned from gold to copper and dipped to touch the clouds in the west. The air was light and sharp; stars pricked through a faded sky.

Glaze looked up at the path, which snaked ahead up the sheer rock side.

He searched for the plateau where the cairn was. No sign of it from here; that meant it was still several hours' climb away. Maybe this deer woman would know.

Schmidt built the fire quickly. As soon as the flames caught, the others moved close. The deer woman watched them for a moment then headed back inside the cave.

'Looks like we found somewhere to stay the night,' Carey whispered.

'She's crazy,' Schmidt said, 'but she's kind. Ain't many would offer to share their supplies.'

'Reckon she's been up here long?' Miller said.

'Too long,' Carey whispered.

The men exchanged glances over the fire. It was safe to risk a joke now the crazy woman was out of earshot.

The deer woman appeared at the mouth of the cave with more wood, larger sticks this time. Going in and out of the narrow opening had knocked the antlers askew; the whole deer head

leaned precariously like some unfin-
ished execution.

'Mind me askin',' Carey said. 'How
come you're up here on your own?' He
was careful not to call her ma'am.

The deer straightened its head so the
antlers reared proudly skywards.

'Came through on a wagon last
winter,' the deer said. 'Got snowed in
on one of the high passes. Couldn't
walk forward or back. Snow was so
deep, took you a day to walk a hundred
yards. Everyone died except me and my
husband. We learned how to survive.'

'How come you didn't come down
when the spring thaw came?' Carey
said.

The antlers dipped as the deer
looked away from him.

'My husband got caught under a
rockfall.' The antlers swayed as the deer
looked out towards the setting sun.
'Busted his legs and ankles real bad.
They never healed up properly. He said
they was getting better but I knew they
wasn't. That fire ready yet?'

The men found reasons to look away. Schmidt busied himself with the kindling; Miller helped him. Glaze stared out across the landscape of cloud at the dying sun.

'I'm sorry,' Carey said.

'Left me his Sharps rifle. He loved that rifle,' the deer said. 'Taught me what I got to do to survive.'

'You seen any wagons since you been up here?' Glaze asked. If this strange creature was minded to talk, he may as well take advantage of it.

The deer glanced at Carey before answering.

'This look like a wagon trail to you?'

'Up on the flat, I meant.'

There was an edge in Glaze's voice. How come this woman talked to Carey and not to him even if she was crazy? The antlers swayed dangerously.

'Ain't been up there for months,' the deer said. 'My husband broke his legs right over there.' She pointed a few yards higher up the path to where a landslip had caused the path to crumble. 'Them rocks fell right on top of him. Anyway, what makes you so full of questions?'

Glaze pressed on.

'We're looking for the Crowleys. Heard they live up here.'

'Crowleys only come up during the wagon season. They all left the mountain weeks ago.' The deer looked contemptuously at him. 'They're robbers. What would be the sense in them staying here when there ain't no wagons?'

The deer turned to Schmidt.

'Fire ready?'

She ducked back inside the cave before he could answer.

Below them, the sun spilled molten copper on to the cloud floor. In the east where the sky had been pale, it was now drained of light; stars peppered the cobalt shadows. The temperature fell; a skin of ice formed over the hats and jackets of the men. They moved closer to the fire.

'A fire and hot food,' Glaze said.

'Could call this a lucky find. Should make the plateau by midday tomorrow.'

The men heard the forced cheerfulness in his voice and stared into the fire.

'When we've got supplies from the cairn, we'll head straight down by the wagon route,' Glaze went on. 'We've just been told the Crowleys are long gone. Any tracks will be under the snow by now.'

He was giving the men good news; they would accomplish their mission and be home within a couple of weeks. But none of them even looked up.

'Sergeant Carey?' Glaze said. He wanted acknowledgement. 'That means we did all we could. The mission will be a success.'

Even as he spoke, Glaze heard how hollow the words sounded.

Carey shut himself behind a wall of army formality; he nodded briefly. 'Lieutenant.'

Even though there was ice on his jacket, Glaze loosened his collar.

The deer edged out of the mouth of

the cave. She had removed her antler helmet but her movements were still cumbersome under the heavy animal skin. Her pinched face was sun-bronzed and dirty with fire smoke; her cheekbones were high and sharp; her lips were thin over black teeth; her small eyes missed nothing. Her dark hair, which contained lines of grey, was pulled back severely and tied with a strip of rag. She held out a blackened skillet with a few thin strips of meat on the bottom.

'You a good shot with that Sharps?' Glaze said.

'Fair,' the deer said. 'My husband was better. He killed this old boy.'

She held out the arm of her coat.

'He killed him and I skinned him. We was a team.'

Schmidt balanced the skillet on the fire. The sharp hiss of fat and the smell of frying turned a claw of hunger in the bellies of the men. Schmidt found a piece of kindling and flipped over the strips of meat. He stared intently into the pan.

The men had never been so hungry. Lack of food had sapped their strength all day. Their heads ached; they felt weak; hunger eroded their resolve. When Glaze talked about the mission achieving success, they could barely summon interest.

The last of the sun plunged below the clouds. The pitch-dark sky was scattered with bright stars. Outside the circle of the fire, the air was freezing. The men moved closer to the flames and the smell of the meat.

Schmidt speared a blackened strip and held it up.

'Who's first?'

Glaze went to take it but the deer's hand darted forward like a claw. She stuffed the dripping meat whole into her mouth. As she chewed, grease spilled down her chin. Schmidt held up a second piece. Glaze took it. Thoroughly charred on all sides, it was impossible to tell what he was holding.

'This some kind of mountain hare?' Glaze said.

'He won't mind what you call him now.' The deer gave a screech of laughter. 'That's my husband.'

8

The skillet leapt out of Schmidt's hand and smashed into the fire. Sparks exploded everywhere. The men threw themselves back from the blaze and swept burning embers off their clothes. Everyone shouted at once; in the struggle to get to their feet, they grabbed wildly at each other for support. Making a dive for the skillet, the deer's shrill laugh cut through the pandemonium and the luxurious smell of burning flesh filled the air.

There was nowhere to go. Back from the fire, the men stared helplessly as the deer grabbed the skillet from the flames and snatched another strip of blackened meat. She ate like a starving animal, barely finishing one mouthful before cramming in the next. Grease ran from the corners of her mouth. She shook her fingers in the air when the iron skillet burned them. Her sharp eyes watched the men as she ate, ready to fight if one of them made a grab for her food.

'Let me look in that cave,' Carey said. 'She's got some mountain dog in there. That's what this is.'

He seized a burning stick from the fire and headed for the narrow opening. Glaze was right behind him.

The two men angled themselves through the split in the rock. Shadows leapt at them in the flickering torch-light. Once through the entrance, the cave widened quickly. The air was still and freezing, colder still than outside. The rock floor was flat and the ceiling domed high above it; in the far distance was the sound of a running stream. Inside the entrance the smell was fetid and overripe. Glaze was reminded of a basket of strawberries that had been left on a window sill until the fruit sank and blue mould bloomed like fur.

Scattered over the floor was the contents of a pioneer's wagon. The filthy canvas bonnet formed a covering for the floor and on it was an old high-backed carver chair, an untidy collection of blankets, cooking pots and a pile of firewood. The Sharps was propped by the entrance; the deer head with its crown of antlers had been left on the chair like a hat politely removed because the wearer had entered a house.

A few steps into the cave, the smell became trenchant. Something had rotted and burst. The further in they went, the stink became deep acrid putrefaction; the men cupped their hands over their mouths and noses.

By the back wall, there were more antlers and a jumble of bones. The stench was unbearable now. Glaze retched; Carey held his hand over his face. The smell came from an untidy pile of uncured hides. A narrow stream appeared out of a crack in the rock on one side of them and disappeared under a pile of stones on the other. A wide-bladed hunting knife had been dropped where someone had been stripping the skins from their carcasses.

Unable to take the stink any longer, the men headed back towards the entrance. As they turned, the light from Carey's torch caught something in the shadows by a side wall. A long slash of white crystal glittered in the dancing flames; at first, Glaze mistook it for a vein of quartz, which a fall of rock had exposed. As they moved closer, they saw it was not crystal but a heap of snow, which someone had brought in from outside. Piled a couple of feet high, it was the width and length of a grave.

Carey moved the torch closer. A human leg had been pulled out from under the snow. Laces trailed from the leather boot still on the foot and the calf was protected by the lower leg of serge pants. Above the knee, the cloth had been cut away and with it, the skin, tissue and muscle of the thigh. There were neat knife marks on the bone where strips of flesh had been taken.

Torchlight flickered over the leg. The men stared for a second, until they understood what they were looking at. They took in the respectful neatness of the cut to the cloth, the even score marks in the thigh bone, the care with which the meat had been cut away. Then they turned, dashed for the entrance and shoved at each other in the struggle to be first outside.

Schmidt and Miller waited on one side of the fire. On the other, the deer woman still held the skillet, swallowed a last mouthful and brushed the grease from her chin into her mouth.

'It's true?' Miller said.

He could tell by the look on Glaze's and the sergeant's face.

'We'll stay out here by the fire,' Glaze mumbled. 'If we leave at first light, we'll make the flats by midday.'

'Reckon the cairn will still be there?' Schmidt said.

'Make up the fire,' Glaze said.

While the deer watched them, she ran her palm round the inside of the

skillet and sucked each finger thought-
fully.

'That's all the wood ration for now,'
she said. 'Fire will last the night if you
don't build it up.'

The men crouched by the flames and
avoided looking at her.

'Sit close,' the deer said. 'I got my
deer skin to keep me warm.'

'There's more hides inside,' Carey
said. 'Stink real bad, though.'

'You're welcome to 'em,' the deer
said kindly. 'Go right in and help
yourselves.'

Schmidt got to his feet.

'Near the back wall,' Carey said.
'Take the torch. I ain't going in there
again.'

When the men were wrapped in the
stinking hides and bedded down by the
fire, Glaze took the first watch.

'Used to make the fire inside the
cave,' the deer said. 'Smoke got so I
couldn't breathe. Now I got my suit, I
don't get cold sitting out here.'

She went back into the cave to collect

her deer head and leaned back against the rock to one side of the mouth of the cave.

Glaze could not bear even to look at this strange creature now, let alone hold a conversation. She repulsed him; he pictured her with her fingers in the skillet and fat spilling out of her mouth. He tried to push out of his mind the image of the human leg which stuck out of the snow pile at the back of the cave with the thigh neatly cut into steaks. Even though hunger gnawed so badly in his belly, he couldn't sleep. For the first time in days, Glaze didn't want to eat. Instead, he stared up at the wide sweep of stars against the black sky.

After an hour, Glaze felt exhaustion get the better of him. One of them had to keep watch. He crawled out from under his animal skin and woke Carey. The others were buried beneath their hides; the deer was still leaning against the rock wall, her antlers sloping precariously. Snow was falling, small flakes, hardly bigger than dust. Glaze shifted the few remaining sticks into the centre of the fire and watched as the flames caught. The air was freezing; each breath turned into ice crystals, which stung his face.

When Glaze next woke, dirty light smeared the eastern sky. It was snowing fast. Like mounds in a churchyard, white heaps showed where the men lay. Carey had fallen asleep; the fire had died; the deer had gone back inside the cave.

Glaze levered himself upright and pulled the hide round his shoulders. He walked over to the others and shook them awake. Then he stooped and gathered up a handful of snow, crammed some in his mouth and rubbed his face with the rest. He hoped this would wake him up but it made him feel worse; the cold burned his mouth while the ice scoured his skin.

The men groaned and stretched themselves into wakefulness. They looked at the falling snow and the dead remains of the fire. As they got to their feet, none of them spoke. The deer angled herself out of the cave, antlers in place.

'You can have our supplies if you go down and find 'em,' Glaze said. 'We need these hides in exchange.'

'Take 'em,' the deer said. She trilled a laugh. 'You starting out now?'

'Right now.' Glaze turned away.

He stared at the falling snow. Gusts of wind swept round the mountain and built white pillows in the lee of the rocks. The fall was relentless. Soon everything would be covered.

Glaze beckoned to the others. With the animal-heavy skin pulled over his head and shoulders and the smell of putrid flesh all about him, he led the way up the path. From the first, his steps were slow and deliberate; each one took effort and concentration. He leaned into the wind; his muscles burned; snow drove into his face. Even turning to check that the others followed was too much effort.

Images of food danced in his head.

He imagined the smell of greasy pork and beans, which used to flood the barracks' cookhouse, breathed it in and savoured its luxury; he tasted the dry salt taste of army issue hard tack in his mouth and held it there until he imagined the flour getting stuck behind his teeth. Best of all was the sweet luxury of sugar candy he remembered from childhood days; he could keep a piece in his mouth for hours until it lay on his tongue like a sliver of bone, the taste of sugar soaked his taste buds and its sweet scent teased his nose.

The higher they climbed, the thicker the snow fell. Glaze walked blind; white flakes careered towards him out of a dark sky. It was impossible to see ahead. His right shoulder bumped against the wall of rock; somewhere to his left ran the edge of the path. Sometimes he could see emptiness and swirling snow, which meant the sheer drop was there; at other times everything was hidden in the wild confusion of the storm and he could not say where the lip of the track was.

One tortured step followed another. Glaze hadn't had feeling in his feet since they started; the wasted muscles in his legs were agony. Locked stiff, his fingers burned where he clutched the hide and the frost-scoured skin of his face itched until he wanted to scratch it off.

Glaze shuffled forward. With the snow knee deep, it was too much effort to pick up each foot, easier to push each step through. The one thought he hung on to was that he had to feel the rock wall against his right shoulder. Sometimes, his lurching steps meant that he swayed out towards the edge of the path; he did not hear the scrape of the animal hide against the rock or feel the jolt of stone against his bruised shoulder. When this happened, panic exploded inside him and he barged into the cliff face while he struggled to correct his steps.

Maybe they had been climbing for an

hour, maybe two; Glaze couldn't tell. In all that time, he had pressed forward step by step with the stinking deer hide pulled tight over his head; he hadn't looked round. He was leading from the front. It was his duty; it was what the men expected. His thoughts drifted back to Bolt: 'I'll bump you up to captain.' The colonel's words clanged hollow like a bell.

The climb was too steep; progress was too slow. They had covered only a few yards in the past hour. At this rate it would take days to reach the plateau where the cairn was and where the food supplies waited for them. For some reason, Glaze had assumed the track would level out, the higher they climbed; in fact, it became steeper. For some reason, he had assumed they would find a rhythm and be able to pace out the climb; in fact, with the blizzard in their faces, their shuffling steps became increasingly awkward and slow.

Glaze thought of the letter in his

pocket; he pictured the perfect copper-plate writing in ink that had once been black but was now beginning to fade; he remembered the warmth of the notepaper in his hands and how easily the sheets fell open along the crease. He imagined how Charlotte had folded the paper with the precise quick movement he had seen her make a hundred times, how she had sharpened a crease with the side of her hand, slipped it into the envelope and turned it over to write his name on the front. His pocket contained this slim object that she had touched with her hands; that made it precious beyond value to him. Whenever he slid the letter out of its envelope and unfolded it flat, it was almost as if he was touching the hand that had written it.

Glaze had reread Charlotte's words so many times, he could recite them. He imagined her chin thrust forward, her tight mouth and the fierce sparkle in her eyes she would have had if she had stood in front of him and spoken the words instead of written them. He pictured the arch of her eyebrows, the line of her auburn hair drawn severely back, the sharpness of her cheekbones and the delicate whiteness of her skin. To the other officers, this showed how frail she was and in need of protection but Glaze knew she was determined and strong. And beautiful. All the officers agreed on that. He knew that whatever happened, he must not let her down.

Colonel Bolt had dispatched his daughter back East two weeks before this mission left the fort. Glaze's request to be part of her escort back to the stage post was denied. Despite his protests, he was ordered out on a routine patrol the day she left. There was no chance to say goodbye.

In his head, Glaze began to recite the words of the letter. As he heard them in his own voice, he pictured each one in Charlotte's copperplate hand right there in front of him as if he were reading it from the page.

'*My dear Calvin, As you are out on a patrol today, I shall not be able to see you to say goodbye . . .*'

Something struck Glaze on the back. At first he thought it was a rock that had fallen from somewhere up the cliff. He pulled the animal hide closer round him and shouldered his way forward into the storm. His right shoulder slammed against the rock; his boots shuffled snow aside.

'*My father reiterated to me the most distressing news of your demotion in rank and became most perturbed and angry when I said you had already made me aware of this. His account of the reason for this drastic action differed so wildly from the account you gave me that I am practically torn in two. I would give anything to be allowed an opportunity to talk this over with you face to face. My poor papa heaped blame upon you most mercilessly . . .*'

Glaze felt another thump against his back. This time he heard someone call his name. He stopped and turned slowly; the hide over his shoulders was frozen stiff. Miller and Schmidt stood there, doubled over under their animal skins. The snow had drifted over them so they looked like great white walking mounds.

Miller was calling to him; Glaze could make out his hoarse cry but the wind snatched his words. They clung to the side of the cliff as snow swirled around them; the sheer drop was obscured by the raging storm. Miller reached out, grabbed the edge of Glaze's animal skin and hauled him close. His cheeks were scrubbed raw by the cold; snow clung to his beard and crusted his eyebrows. His face twisted with the effort of shouting against the wind but his words were faint.

'It's the sarge.'

Glaze leaned forward to catch what he was saying. Snow leaped and danced between them.

'Sergeant Carey's gone.'

Glaze pulled away from him. Schmidt

stood behind him, a hulking snow pile with the storm battering round him. Glaze could just make out his face under the animal skin; like Miller, he was bearded with crystals of snow.

Glaze stared over Schmidt's shoulder to where Carey should be. There was nothing, just emptiness and the wild snow raging on the wind.

9

'Where is he?'

Panic gripped Glaze's lungs and made it impossible to breathe. Choking, he stared into Miller's face; words caught in his throat. The weight of the hide heaped with snow bent his back. Now that he was still, fire burned the muscles of his legs; he slumped against the rock wall, too weak to support his own weight.

He stared over Schmidt's shoulder, desperate for some sight of the sergeant. He was there, he must be. Maybe Glaze had set too fast a pace and Carey's leg had made him fall behind. Maybe he couldn't keep up and he had stopped to rest. Thoughts cannoned into each other inside Glaze's head. As he stared back down where the direction of the track lay, snowflakes dived and danced as though the entire sky mocked his foolishness and blamed him for the missing man.

The wind made a single eerie note against the rock walls of the ravine, a long chime, which resonated and hung in the air. It made the men peer into the storm as though something was calling them; it reminded them of how far away they were from everything they knew. It made them look from one to the other to reassure themselves that they were not alone.

Then the wind switched direction; the sound died. The men were left staring into the skirling snow.

'Where is he?' Glaze repeated.

He beckoned Schmidt to come close.

'He was behind me,' Schmidt said. 'That's all I know.'

Glaze felt the men's eyes on him. They were waiting for him to decide.

'Maybe he went back,' Miller said.

What was he saying? Glaze stared at him. Was he taunting him? Was he saying that the sergeant had deserted? What nonsense was this?

'Could have gone back to that deer woman,' Miller said.

Glaze could barely hear his words above the cry of the wind.

There was mockery in Miller's eyes, Glaze thought. And contempt. Miller resented all officers. Now his resentment had turned to blame and his blame had turned to hatred.

'What?' Glaze still didn't understand.

'Maybe he went back to eat,' Miller said. 'You wouldn't let us go back for the supplies.'

'Eat?'

Carey would never do that. Just the thought of it horrified Glaze. Not Sergeant Carey, who somehow had the knack of earning the respect of the officers and the affection of the men. Not his sergeant, who always carried out orders to the letter and never complained.

'Gonna put him on a charge, too?' Miller said.

'You're talking nonsense, Private.'

Glaze had to front it out. But behind

the show of officer's indignation, a doubt was sown. Miller knew Carey; he wasn't stupid. Had the two of them talked about this? Had they decided something between them?

'Even suggesting . . . ' Glaze continued.

'We gonna go back, Lieutenant?' Schmidt interrupted.

'Go back?' Glaze stared at him. Under the animal skin, Schmidt's face was pinched and grey. The edges of his eyes were red and snow was caught in his beard.

The snow swirled in front of Glaze's eyes and blew into his face. Earlier the cold had made his face itch until he had wanted to claw it off with his bare hands; now he couldn't feel anything. He knew the snow must be catching in his beard and landing against his skin but he couldn't feel it. The wind had frozen his skin.

'To look for him,' Schmidt said.

'He's dead, got blown off the edge,' Miller said. 'Or else he went back to the deer woman. Either way there ain't no point in looking for him.'

'We wait,' Glaze said. 'Give him time to catch up. He could have fallen or slowed to take a rest. If he don't come then we carry on.'

'He ain't coming,' Miller said. 'Either way.'

Glaze ignored the insubordination. Now he had made a decision, he felt his strength return. He stared out into the storm. They were due for a rest, anyway.

The men sank down onto the track, leaned back against the rock wall and listened to the cry of the wind. Each time Glaze looked into either of their faces, he recognized them less. Their eyes were bloodshot; snow caked their beards and eyebrows; their cheeks were sunk in and their blotchy skin seemed sewn together out of patches.

As the storm and its leaden sky blocked out the sun, the men lost track of time. Had they been walking for an hour or two or even three? And how far? The snow lying on the narrow track got thicker as they climbed until every pace they took was slower and cost more effort than the last. As they couldn't see ahead to the flats, they couldn't tell how much further they had to go.

The men pulled the animal skins around them and closed their eyes. The little strength they had left dissolved into exhausted sleep. The snow fell on them and they didn't notice; the wind moaned and they didn't hear it; the cold would have numbed their hands and feet but already they had no feeling left.

Sometime later, Miller shook the others awake. He pulled the hide off Glaze's head, brushed away the snow and grabbed his shoulders. Glaze became aware of this angry figure with a blistered face leaning over him, shouting something against the wind. The storm was worse.

Glaze knew in his mind where he was. He knew he had to force himself to his feet; he knew if he stayed there for much longer he would freeze to death — they all would. But he had no desire to make even the slightest effort to move. It was like floating. He could stay there forever, the storm could blow around him, the snow could rage and he would just lie there hunched over inside his animal skin. He would be numb and nothing would matter because he could feel nothing.

Miller dragged him to his feet. He spat words in Glaze's face but Glaze couldn't make them out. Miller shook him and yelled again. The wind soared, its cry rising to a scream; snow flew in great arcs, which obliterated the sky. Ahead, the track was buried; a few yards back, Schmidt still lay on the path.

That was what Miller was telling him. Something about Schmidt. Glaze stared into Miller's exasperated face. Then Glaze's brain seemed to pick up speed again and he could hear Miller's words against the shout of the wind.

Schmidt wouldn't move. They had to get him upright. They had to make him walk. Glaze took a step towards where Schmidt lay under a snow pile; while they slept, the storm had buried them alive.

'Private Schmidt,' Glaze yelled.

Inside his head, he heard his voice hoarse and strained; he hardly recognized himself. He leaned down and heaved at Schmidt's huge shoulder. It was like trying to shift a frozen buffalo. Glaze thought he was dead.

Then Schmidt's eyelids flickered open. He looked at Glaze but saw nothing; his eyes were as empty as water. Glaze shook him and shouted. Schmidt tried to lift his head. The wind whipped round them; each time they brushed snow away from Schmidt's face, the wind showered it again.

Glaze saw how the colour of Schmidt's face had changed. Where exhaustion had formerly left the skin grey, now there were patches of sickly yellow edged with the colour of blood.

To the touch, the surface of his skin was as crisp as sugar.

'Private Schmidt.' Glaze leaned over him and yelled in his ear. 'This is an order.'

Glaze heard Miller laugh.

'You ordering him to stay alive?'

Schmidt moved his arm to push Glaze away. He heaved himself up; it took time for him to realize where he was.

'We're moving out right now,' Glaze said. 'We'll die if we stay here.'

Schmidt lumbered to his feet. He pulled at Glaze's shoulder and spoke in his ear; his voice was scarcely a whisper.

'Where's the sarge?'

Glaze turned from him and looked back down where the track had been. It was filled with snow and indistinguishable from the rock side. He couldn't tell its width or even where exactly it lay. Up ahead, the track had also disappeared. All they could do was hug the cliff and work their way along.

'Where's the sarge?' Schmidt repeated. 'Come on.'

Glaze pulled the animal skin over his head and beckoned Schmidt to follow. He stared down at his feet. There was no point in trying to see the path ahead; if he looked up, the wind flayed his face. He kept the cliff side jolting against his shoulder and pushed his boots into the snow.

The track was steep. Pain screwed the muscles of his legs tight and drove nails into his knees. The animal hide ploughed behind him in the snow; the extra weight hauled against his shoulders. The wind headed into him like a train.

Glaze's mind wandered. The air was hot and the sun was bright. Newly posted to Fort Brandish as a captain, he was riding the plains at the head of his first patrol. His heart was light; he wanted to laugh out loud with the joy of it. His head was full of the sound of hoofs pounding over the dry ground; the air was full of dust and the stink of trampled sage. The sun beat down.

Glaze's throat was parched and his skin burned. The men had been riding for hours. He knew they were tired; he knew the horses needed rest; he himself ached with fatigue. But none of this mattered. He wore hardship like a badge of honour; it was proof that he was doing his duty and doing it right. He would be able to return to the fort and look his colonel in the eye and say he had done his utmost. Pride and praise would be his.

Up ahead, floating on the heat haze were the white bonnets of a line of covered wagons. Captain Glaze led his unit towards them. These were the pioneers who were settling this great country in the West and Captain Glaze was leading his men to make the trail safe for them. The thunder of hoof beats, the jingle of bridles, the smell of saddle leather and horses' sweat, the power of the cavalry horse he rode all combined in the blaze of golden sunlight to make him feel invincible.

Right was on his side; he was strong and he was good.

And in his heart was a picture, a picture of a pretty, young girl. Knowing it was there filled Glaze with exalting pleasure; it reassured him of the rightness of his cause. It made him drive his men hard because he drove himself hard. He did this to feel worthy of the young woman, the colonel's daughter with whom he had an understanding.

A lieutenant pulled up alongside him. Glaze did not slow his horse. He knew this lieutenant. He was younger than Glaze, still wet behind the ears. He expected him to advise that the men needed rest, to counsel caution when approaching the train, to advise that someone be sent out on point.

'Sir?' the lieutenant shouted.

Glaze looked across as though he had just realized he was there. It amused him to see the young officer try to shout to him as they galloped together.

'What is it, Lieutenant?'

If anything, Glaze quickened his speed. The warm wind in his face, the flashing sunlight, the pulse of the horses' hoof beats made his heart race. Why should he slow down so a junior officer could counsel caution?

'Suggest we separate the unit, sir.' The lieutenant was breathless. 'Approach in a pincer.'

'Reason for your advice, Lieutenant?' Glaze was enjoying this. It would make a good tale for the Mess. Stories about how junior officers were wrong-footed always raised a laugh.

'Wagon train's not moving, sir.'

Glaze stared hard. Heat twisted the air. The line of bonnets shimmered in the haze. He couldn't tell.

'Trains always form a circle when they take their nooning stop,' the lieutenant went on.

The wind chopped from one side of the ravine to the other and hurled snow in the faces of the men. They dug their boots in the snow and stopped. The incline was sharper now and the snow on the path deeper. The effort was too much.

Glaze fell against the rock wall; every fibre of him screamed to be allowed to lie down. His body tried to trick him. Let me lie down for a little while, just until I'm rested, until the burning stops in my legs, until my strength returns. Let me sleep; if I can sleep, just for a few minutes, when I wake all my strength will come back.

Schmidt, head bowed against the driving snow, cannoned into him and almost sent him sprawling. Miller was close behind. The two men stared at him. The deer skins over their heads were piled with snow.

'Carey?' Glaze said.

Behind Miller, the snow careered away into a void. Glaze heard him say something but his voice was too faint for Glaze to catch. Miller grabbed the edge of Glaze's hide and hauled him close. Miller's hands were raw; the swellings on his face were the colour of shadows.

'What are you saying?' Miller's words scraped from his throat.

What was he saying? Glaze stared into Miller's blistered face. He didn't know. Something had made him turn to look for Carey but now he couldn't say what it was. Miller turned to Schmidt but the wind snatched his words. They both leaned close and stared at Glaze as if they were examining him for something.

'Carey's dead.' Glaze felt Miller's breath on his face. 'Or he turned back. What are you asking about him for?'

'Dead?' Glaze said.

He knew but he had forgotten. Of course he knew.

A picture of the young lieutenant riding alongside him came into Glaze's head; he shouted something to him over the drum of the horses' hoofs. The line of white wagon bonnets shimmered in the midday heat. The lieutenant's face was anxious; Glaze remembered the young man's cautious advice and how he ignored it. Instead, he laughed in the sunshine at the exhilaration of the ride.

'What did you stop for?' Miller grabbed him again.

The blinding snow swerved in on the wind and charged at them headlong; the squall pitched itself against the sides of the ravine. Glaze turned and heaved another step forward into the snow on the rocky path.

10

Glaze walked blind. When he stumbled he knew there were frozen rocks beneath the snow but as his feet were numb he couldn't feel himself kick against them. If his toes were broken, he couldn't tell.

Sometimes he tripped and pitched face forward. It didn't take much to topple any of them. The snow hiding obstructions on the path, the wind battering them and the weight of the hides made them unsteady. Every time he fell, he wanted to lie there and not get up; every time he levered himself to his feet, he thought the effort would use up the last of his strength. Until he took a step. And another. Then, somehow, his legs took on the leaden rhythm of pushing into the snow again and he shuffled blindly forward while his thoughts took on the quality of dreams.

Up ahead, the line of wagons dipped and rose on the waves of sage and buffalo grass. Hard sunlight glinted off the silver-grey leaves as the wind moved across the surface of the plain. As the cavalry horses powered forward, their hoof beats rolled like summer thunder. Light flashed off the troopers' buttons, caught their epaulettes, and gleamed on their polished boots. At the gallop, keeping pace with Glaze, the young lieutenant had a look of controlled patience on his face. He tried again.

'Sir.'

Glaze turned to him.

'Something ain't right,' the lieutenant insisted.

Glaze nodded and raised his hand to halt the troopers who followed him. He spoke to his horse and pulled back on the reins. The drum roll of hoofs eased and the brown dust kicked up by the horses settled in the air.

'What is it, Lieutenant?'

Glaze could see that the fellow was doing his best; he wanted him to feel that he took account of his opinions. It would build loyalty if he was seen to do that in front of the men, especially as this was his first summer on the plains.

'The men are saying we ought to form a pincer; it's what we always do.'

Glaze's easy smile fell from his face. He ran a finger around the collar of his shirt as if it was suddenly too tight.

'The men?' Glaze said.

He stared at the lieutenant and waited for an explanation.

'In the past we've approached in a pincer,' the lieutenant said again. 'Or sent out a scout.'

'It's a wagon train, Lieutenant.' Glaze shaded his eyes and stared ahead. 'Pure and simple.'

'Seen this before, sir. Wagons stopped in a line,' the lieutenant went on. 'Volunteer to go in as a scout, sir.'

'Appreciate that, Lieutenant,' Glaze said. He kept his eyes fixed on the wagons. The horses were still in their traces; the train must be just about to pull out. 'Won't be necessary.'

'With respect, sir, the land looks flat here but it ain't. Could be an ambush waiting for us. If I rode ahead — '

Glaze cut him off. What they said about junior officers in the Mess was right. They didn't know when to button it.

'Thank you, Lieutenant,' Glaze said stiffly.

Then he remembered what Colonel Bolt had told him about a settling-in period. 'You're new, officer. It will take a while for the men to get used to you. Give them time. Listen to what they have to say.' Hadn't he done just that? Glaze kept his eyes on the wagons. 'At the end of the day, remember you're in charge,' Bolt had said.

There was nothing untoward, Glaze was sure of it. The sea of waving grass, the hard blue sky and the line of wagons — there was nothing else. He strained his eyes to see if the wagons had started to move, but the air danced and stretched in the midday heat and he couldn't tell.

Glaze raised his hand again ready to signal to the column to move forward. The horses' hoofs bit into the hard ground; the sunlight flashed on brass and polished leather. The young lieutenant fell back and left Captain Glaze at the head of the column.

It was a mile to the wagons, Glaze judged. He glanced over his shoulder; the lieutenant was immediately behind him and the men followed in tight formation. Glaze spurred his horse; his heart leapt.

The ground started to fall away. At its full summer height, the sagebrush disguised a dip in the land. As the column charged down it, they lost sight of the wagon train. Terror ran through Glaze. His heart exploded against his ribs; he gripped the reins until his knuckles burst. What if the lieutenant was right? What if there was an ambush? He said he had seen this before. He told him about the unevenness of the ground; he had volunteered to go in on point.

As Glaze pushed his horse up the opposite slope to the crest of the rise, he expected the Apocalypse. His tunic choked him; he couldn't breathe. He looked round and the lieutenant was there, right behind him. Glaze drew his pistol ready to take a shot at the first living thing he saw. He would be an easy target; for a second he would be the only one on level ground until the lieutenant and the men caught up. He would be the first one to die.

Glaze's horse heaved itself over the edge of the rise. Alone against the skyline, he was a marksman's gift. He urged his horse on, waiting out the long seconds while the men climbed after him, waiting for the shot.

As he pressed forward, he felt the sun on his face; the shot didn't come. The glorious thought came to him. 'I was right.' He would include an account of it in his official report for the colonel. Told differently, it would be another story for the Officers' Mess. Pride reared in him again.

The rise and fall of the land didn't bother him now. If the wagons dipped out of sight and then reappeared, it meant nothing. There was no ambush; there was no need for the young lieutenant's caution.

Overcaution caused the men to lose confidence; that was something else he would consider for his report.

It was odd that no one from the wagons came out to greet them. The pioneers would have heard the rumble of their horses' hoofs some time ago; they would have seen the standard above the sage and caught the sun flashing off the bridles. Where were they? Glaze raised his hand again to slow the column.

The wagons were in a perfect line, nose to tail along the Emigrant Road. The lighter wagons were at the front of the column with mules harnessed; the ones drawn by oxen were further back. The animals seemed content enough. The mules ducked their heads to graze on the buffalo grass; the oxen ruminated peacefully. From thirty yards out, Glaze noticed a single arrow bedded in the tailboard of one of the wagons. He slowed his horse.

The lieutenant rode up alongside; he'd seen the arrow, too.

Glaze called out to announce himself.

'Captain Glaze, Mounted Rifles. Coming in.'

No reply. The lieutenant brought the troopers to a halt.

It was an ideal opportunity. He would go in himself in full view of the men. They would see him ride point; they would see how he kept a cool head. His courage would inspire confidence.

'Have the men form a line parallel with the wagons, facing the train,' Glaze said to the lieutenant.

The men lined up as Glaze walked his horse towards the wagons. It took an age. The air hummed with heat; he heard the jingle of his bridle and the swish of sagebrush against the legs of his horse. He felt the eyes of the men on his back.

When Glaze reached the first wagon, he called out. No answer. His grip tightened on his pistol as he cut in behind the wagon and leaned over the tailboard. Neatly tied down were the usual pieces of furniture, a heap of folded bedding, the water barrel and sacks of supplies.

Everything was in perfect order. As he pulled his horse clear and moved on to the next wagon, a pair of mules turned their heads towards him. They studied him briefly while they dealt flies a lazy flick of their tails. Pleased with the example he was setting, Glaze worked his way along the length of the train. All the wagons were empty.

When he reached the last one, something on the far side of the line of wagons caught his attention. Glaze looked back. The line of troopers stared at him. It was only a few yards; it would look foolish to call for assistance now. He rode forward.

The body of a girl lay face down amongst the sage. A bloodstain darkened the back of her dress. Her head was unnaturally twisted to one side where she had fallen. Her face was suntanned and delicate; there was blood on her lips and her eyes were closed. Her dark pigtail was flung to one side; the strings of bright beads she wore round her neck were spread out across the sage. She was beautiful.

The wind wheeled round the men. One moment, it pitched them against the rock wall, the next it threatened to barge them off the edge of the track. The snow was wild and directionless, thicker than before. The men clung to the edge of the mountain and shuffled on, step by step. When Glaze peered round, he could just make out the shapes of Miller and Schmidt, dark hulks, their faces hidden by the animal hides.

The track was steeper again. Glaze's legs burned; his lungs were bursting. He was desperate to lie down. The snow on the path was soft and inviting. The wind made voices in his head, telling him to slow down, there was no need to carry on, he should lie down right where he was and rest.

Miller cannoned into him and toppled him over. Glaze hadn't realized he had come to a standstill. The fall into the snow drift was gentle; lying down was like floating; the snowflakes that landed on his face calmed him. Within seconds he was giving himself up to sleep.

Then Miller was shaking him. What was the matter with the man? Couldn't he see Glaze wanted him to let him be? Miller was angry. As he gazed up into his face, Glaze could see that. He was shouting but whether it was the wind flinging his words away or whether his voice was hoarse now, Glaze couldn't make out what he was saying. His words sounded as if they were coming from somewhere far away.

Miller pulled at him. Now Schmidt was there, too. Together they hauled him back onto his feet. The animal hide slipped off his shoulders; Glaze saw it fall at his feet. Freezing wind slashed through his clothes until he hauled the skin back over his head.

Behind him, Glaze heard Miller shout again. His right shoulder slammed against the rock wall and he forced himself to take another step. The wind shrieked and the snow did its mocking dance in front of his face. His feet slipped on frozen stones under the snow and he stumbled again. The track was getting steeper.

11

For hours the wind barged headlong into Glaze and the others, switched direction and shouldered them repeatedly into the rock face. It played with the leaden animal skins, which they pulled over their heads, ballooned them as if they were silk scarves and tugged them out of the men's frozen fingers. All this time, a wall of snow ran at them and blinded them when they tried to see ahead. The men dropped their shoulders, stared at their feet and willed themselves to take each shuffling step. They had no feeling in their feet and fingers; they could no longer feel the scourge of frozen snow against their cheeks.

They were now used to the claustrophobic twilight in which the blizzard raged. Neither day nor night, the snow attacked them out of grey, half-light.

The dull monochrome had no connection to where the sun was in the sky. The storm created its own world where light was semi-darkness, the wind screamed in pain and the air froze. It deprived the men of their senses; it was a world without end or beginning.

Suddenly, something changed. The snow skirled round the men in huge circles and attacked them from all sides. Their legs almost gave way under them as the contour of the land under their feet levelled out. The shrill note of the wind against the rock face sank to a moan.

Glaze turned to the others. He wanted to speak but the inside of his throat had turned to paper. Miller shuffled close.

'This it?'

Glaze nodded.

Schmidt stared wildly round, searching for a shape that might be the cairn. Here, just as on the path, the endless, swirling, white blizzard engulfed him and only allowed him to see a few feet ahead. He toppled towards the others.

'Whereabouts is it?' Schmidt's voice was broken and desperate.

Glaze remembered a neat triangle of stones at one edge of the plateau beside the parallel ruts of wagon wheels in the spring grass; it stood on the west side where the view of the high peaks stretched to the horizon. He stared round him at the drifted snow. When he took a pace forward, he sank up to his waist.

'On the west side.'

He waved an arm vaguely. Schmidt fell in behind him and they began to plough through the drifts in the direction Glaze thought west might be. Already exhausted, the effort of forcing their way forward was too much. Schmidt sank down; the others saw how hopeless the task was and joined him. In a hollow in the snow, at least they were out of the wind.

'One of us stays awake,' Glaze said. 'The others can sleep.'

Schmidt felt for his army issue knife

and sawed a piece off his frozen deer skin; when he put it in his mouth, the ice tore away part of his lips. Glaze drew his legs up and watched the snow settle on his companions. Miller's eyes closed right away.

Glaze stared at Miller's blistered face. There were purple swellings across his cheeks and under his eyes; in places, freezing air scoured the skin away and red sores broke through. His beard was frozen and snowflakes rested on his eyelashes. Sleep kidnapped him as soon as he closed his eyes; he was used up.

Schmidt chewed feebly to try and soften the piece of deer hide in his mouth. His face was raw and blistered like Miller's. Where he clutched at the animal skin, Glaze could see that the ends of his fingers were black.

Snow danced mockingly over them as night fell. The grey fog-light, which had surrounded them since morning, now slipped away. Glaze struggled to stay awake; he knew snow was burying them but he could not see it. Blackness surrounded him.

He felt for the letter inside his jacket; just to touch the paper with the tips of his fingers would give him some strength. But the cold had drawn all feeling out of his hand; he knew he had pushed it inside his coat but he couldn't feel it there. He wondered if his fingers were black like Schmidt's but, lying in a daze of semi-wakefulness, did not have the strength to feel concerned. He was curious, that was all. As his thoughts drifted, inside his head he saw the sunshine on the plains.

The day was bright and the midday heat sang in the sage. The little girl's body lay in front of him. She had been facing away from the wagon train when somebody shot her. Instinctively, Glaze slipped down from his saddle to check if she was alive. 'Running away,' he thought. He looked around for something she might have stolen but there was nothing. Her hand still held a headdress of partridge feathers she had made. The sight of the girl's body rattled him. If it were not for the bloodstain on the back of her dress, he would have said she was sleeping.

Ahead of him the sage was broken down. Glaze glanced back at the troopers lined up on the other side of wagons. He climbed back up onto his horse and rode slowly forward. The brush was thick here; he had to let the horse pick its way through. The sun beat on his shoulders. He couldn't get the image of the girl out of his head; she must have been no more than six years old. The sun made Glaze's head ache; up ahead, heat bent the air.

Glaze wanted to be on his way. If the wagons were deserted, he would report it back at the fort; his patrol was too small to do much about it. Then his heart leapt. Lying in the sage was a child's toy, the kind of thing everyone gave their sons as soon as they were old enough to walk, a piece of wood carved into the shape of a rifle.

'Must have come from one of the

wagons,' Glaze thought. But his mind was still on the Indian girl. Something about her had got to him.

He remembered the complaints about the pioneers he had heard almost every day since he was posted to the fort. 'They come out West and don't know nothing about the frontier,' was one. 'Mention the word Sioux and you see them reach for their rifles,' was another. 'It's always us that has to clean up the mess.'

The line of wagons was seventy yards back. Glaze could make out the troopers waiting on the other side.

Up ahead the leaves of a cottonwood tree shook in the warm breeze. At its roots, a spring broke through the dry earth and formed a shallow pool. It occurred to Glaze that he could get the men to refill their canteens. He moved forward to check whether the water was good.

Shortly after that, Glaze saw the bodies. Men and women from the wagon train. All with their throats cut.

Their limbs were twisted into impossible angles; they looked as though a whirlwind had snatched them up and dumped them; some still held pails in their hands. Blood had rained on the sage where they lay.

Glaze did not trust himself not to throw up. He allowed himself to glance down at the body nearest him. It was a man, thin-faced and tall, in a blood-spattered work shirt. A rifle was discarded beside him. His head was thrown back and fat flies inspected the gash in his neck. His dead eyes stared.

Glaze started to wheel his horse; his hand pulled back the hammer on his Colt. Before he could draw, a Sioux brave sprang out of the brush and cannoned him out of his saddle. Glaze's skull slammed against the baked earth. The brave hurled himself on top of him and pinned him down. He knelt on Glaze's chest and pressed a knife across his windpipe with one hand while with the other he knocked Glaze's gun out of his hand and flung it away into the sage.

The brave's eyes were alight with anger. He was strong; Glaze's age, maybe. The man's weight crushed him; Glaze couldn't breathe. He waited for the sharp sideways motion of the knife.

Then, with his eyes fixed on Glaze's face, the brave shifted his weight and lifted the knife slightly to allow air into his lungs. While Glaze choked, the brave grabbed a handful of his hair and with the knife still tight against his throat, hauled him to his feet. The brave turned him to face the line of wagons.

Beyond them the troopers were being pulled off their horses. In one coordinated movement, Sioux fighters leapt up from the brush, slashed the soldiers' throats and hauled them backwards out of their saddles. Only the braves got to their feet again.

Glaze writhed and tried to shout. With his head yanked back, he felt the blade nick his skin and a line of blood run down his neck. The brave held him until it was clear all the troopers were dead. It was over in seconds. Then he kicked Glaze's legs away from under him and sent him sprawling in the brush. As he started to walk away, he tossed something down beside Glaze. It was the headdress of partridge feathers.

As Glaze jolted awake, panic shuddered through him. The face of the Sioux brave stared at him. And something held his eyes shut. For a moment he thought he was blind. Then he realized that snow had frozen his eyelashes together. He rubbed his face and eyes and blinked them open.

Blackness. He shouldn't have let himself fall asleep. But the others hadn't noticed. He leaned out of the animal hide and felt in the darkness, just to check that they were still there. He couldn't even tell whether it was still snowing.

Glaze had no strength left at all. Everything was a monumental effort. Just summoning the energy to remember he had to wake Miller exhausted him; crawling the few feet near enough to shake him was too much. He fell back in the snow. Then, for some reason, he remembered Schmidt's black fingernails; he pictured the broken blisters on Miller's face.

Glaze's old fears came back to spook him. The men would blame him for this, wouldn't they? They would blame him for making them go on; they would say any other officer would have turned back and abandoned the mission. They would say so back at the fort. Like always, gossip would spread and eventually Bolt would hear it.

Suddenly his official report would not be enough and Bolt would call him in for questioning. Everyone would say it was his fault when all he had done was follow orders. Being questioned was like being accused and being accused was like being found guilty. Everyone would know.

Glaze collapsed on top of Miller. Then he realized it must still be snowing; there was a pile a foot deep on Miller's body. He did his best to shake him, did his best to call out his name. His tongue bent like a claw in his throat; he was barely able to utter a sound. Miller didn't move.

The thought came to Glaze that because he had fallen asleep, Miller's blood had frozen in his veins and he was dead. Glaze knew he had to keep shaking him; this would get his blood flowing again. He brushed away the snow, pulled back the hide and shook Miller's shoulders. He called out his name in his desiccated, claw voice.

Eventually, Miller stirred.

'That you, Sarge?' His voice was weak and cracked in his throat.

'It's me,' Glaze said. 'You're on watch.'

Miller groaned.

'Is it still snowing?'

12

'Still snowing?'

The words swirled in Glaze's brain. At first he thought he hadn't slept at all — his body was numb. Then he realized he was lying in a pool of ice water. His clothes were soaked; melted snow dripped off his hat and splashed his face like rain. So weak he was barely able to make the effort to open his eyes, he tried to angle his head so that the water fell on his parched lips but the movement knocked his hat sideways and the stream of water ran down his neck and jolted him awake.

Bright sunshine lanced down into the hollow. Everywhere, snow thawed. The lip of the crater where they slept had dissolved; the piles of snow that had built up on the men as they slept had been eaten away. The animal skin Glaze had pulled round him had unfolded during the night and held the lake of rust-coloured water in which he lay. The stink of decay had returned to it.

Glaze forced himself to sit up. His movements were slow and stiff, as if his muscles were still frozen. He slipped backwards and snow fell in his face.

When Glaze managed to lever himself up on to one elbow, he saw two snowy mounds, which had lain beside him all night. Half buried under the hides, they looked like dead animals that hunters had left behind. Neither moved; a shard of panic twisted in him in case Miller and Schmidt were dead and he was alone. He tried to call to them, but the effort of trying to shout left him breathless.

Miller was nearest. Glaze leaned across and pulled back the animal hide that covered his face. His cheeks were bruised and chapped; skin flaked off his lips until they were raw. His head was drenched where snow had melted in his hair.

'Miller.'

Glaze's voice was barely a whisper. The shard turned again, faster this time. In his head he imagined Colonel Bolt demanding to know what had happened, demanding to know who was on watch, demanding to know how it could be that all his men were dead. As the colonel's iron face leaned over him, Glaze had no answers. Despite his wet, freezing clothes he felt sweat prick the back of his neck.

Miller groaned; his eyes flickered open and then closed again. The lids were swollen and red.

'Miller.' Glaze's voice cracked.

He grabbed Miller's shoulder. Miller's eyes opened again and he pushed himself upright. His clothes were soaked; he had been lying in a similar pool inside his hide. When he saw the sunshine, his mouth twisted into a smile.

'Where's Schmidt?' Miller's voice caught in his throat.

It was such a foolish question, it

took Glaze by surprise. Schmidt was lying right there. He was going to wake him next. For some reason, Miller hadn't understood. As Glaze started to explain, Miller reached over and pulled back Schmidt's hide. The loose pile of snow that covered it fell aside.

'Where is he?' Miller repeated.

Glaze now saw that the side of the crater they had slept in had been newly broken down. The men helped each other to stand. Their joints cracked and muscles tore in their legs. They blinked back the sharpness of the sunshine and stared round them at the snow-covered plateau. Hunger Flats.

All around, snow-covered peaks reared into the blue sky and above them trails of cirrus cloud caught the sun. At one end of the plateau the entrance to the wagon trail was guarded by a stand of towering ponderosa pines. At the opposite end, the start of the climb towards the high pass disappeared into a wall of boulders.

The western edge of the plateau was

separated from them by an acre of shining snow. There was no sign of a cairn above the drifts but the top of Schmidt's head was visible; he had ploughed a furrow direct from where he had slept. Stoked with energy at the thought of the cairn, Glaze headed towards him; Miller followed. They tried to call out but the effort of pushing through the snow made them catch their breath. Even softened by the morning sun, the drifts were still waist deep.

As they stumbled nearer, they heard Schmidt cursing to himself. He flung handfuls of stones aside and kicked at the base of the cairn to try to dislodge it. As they got there, the ice cracked as the last of the stones came loose under his feet.

'Schmidt?' Glaze called. 'Found anything?'

Schmidt stood up suddenly. He was wild-eyed; his face was beaten from where the cold had got under his skin. He had flung aside the animal hide and his jacket and had been tearing at the stones in his shirt sleeves. He held a rock wrenched from the cairn in bloody fingers. There was something, which looked like mud, caught in his beard.

'What have you found?' Miller's words tore at his throat. 'I know you. What have you found?'

He shoved Glaze aside and blundered towards Schmidt through the snow.

The big man stood there with his arms by his sides, a blank expression on his tortured face as if he heard the words but didn't understand. For a moment, Glaze thought Miller was going to launch himself at Schmidt like he had done further back down the mountain. He stumbled after him.

At Schmidt's feet, stones were scattered around wildly in the trodden snow. A piece of oilcloth, which had formed the outer wrapping of a parcel, lay open; it had been wiped clean.

'What's that?' Miller yelled.

He grabbed Schmidt by the shoulders and shook him.

'What have you done?'

'Hard tack,' Schmidt said helplessly. 'But the water got into it. Turned it back to flour.'

'You ate it?' Miller had Schmidt by the throat. 'You ate it all?'

'Wasn't no good.' Schmidt struggled to tear Miller's hands away. 'Water got into it.'

'What about us?' Miller's voice was like the screech of a bird.

Glaze pulled Miller off.

'You ate it all?' Glaze's voice was hollow.

He stared around at the detritus of stones. There were no more parcels. Thoughts cannoned into each other inside his head. He drew his Colt.

'You ate the supplies?' Glaze's voice shook.

He pulled back the hammer.

'You did that?'

Schmidt stared at him as though he had asked him a question he didn't understand. He hung his head. He looked lost. His arms fell helplessly by his side. Blood dripped from his fingers and made tiny red discs on the snow.

'Shoot him,' Miller yelled.

He made a grab for Glaze's gun.

'I'll do it. You ain't got the belly for it.'

Glaze pulled the trigger. The sound of the shot bounced across the frozen plateau. Schmidt fell back into the snow; a dark patch decorated the chest of his grey army shirt like a medal.

Miller picked up the piece of oil cloth, held it up to the sunshine and peered at it.

'He licked it clean,' he said.

He threw the cloth down in disgust.

Glaze slowly replaced the Colt in his holster. He sank down into a snowdrift; the strength it took to stand was too much. He pulled the stinking deer hide around him, suddenly aware of the cold. His clothes and the inside of the hide were soaking wet. His teeth rattled in his skull and his whole body shook.

He cast his eyes over Schmidt's body and almost envied him.

Miller watched him.

'Don't you worry, Lieutenant,' he said. 'Anyone would have done the same.'

Glaze didn't look up. Miller wasn't sure that he had heard him.

'I'll find wood for a fire,' Miller said. 'I'll build a real big fire that'll keep us warm all day.'

He turned and stumbled through the snow in the direction of the pines.

Glaze sat there for a while after Miller had gone. He fixed his gaze on the patch of ground in front of him and kept his eyes from straying to look at Schmidt's body. He stared at snow blackened with dirt and scattered with stones and thought of nothing. He had shot one of his own men. He couldn't allow himself to think. There would be a court martial; the regiment would disown him; Bolt would recommend him for a firing squad. He imagined Charlotte's sweet face. How could he admit what he had done?

Miller was far away now, a tiny figure close to the edge of the pines. After he watched him disappear into the trees, Glaze pushed himself to his feet. He took a few leaden steps over to the patch of bare earth where the cairn had stood. He knelt down and ran his hand over it inch by inch, checking to see if there was anything buried. He brushed the snow away and prised up the few remaining stones. There was nothing. Just ice, rock and frozen dirt.

When he moved the oilcloth, something caught his eye. A piece of slate with awkward letters scratched on it was trodden into the snow. 'Last of our hard tack. All we can spare. Hungry ourselves. Good Luck. Justine Weaver, 5 December 1847.'

Glaze put the slate down carefully beside him. The bones of the Weaver family had been found in one of the high passes by the first wagon to cross the mountains last spring. The story of how their wagon had been discovered snowed in with a broken axle shocked the fort. Their supplies had run out. Their mules starved. When they realized the snow was too deep for them to be able to carry on or go back on foot, they ate the scrawny mules and burned the contents of the wagon to keep warm. Sometime after that, to prevent themselves from giving up all hope, they burned the wagons. Their bones were found picked clean a mile further west. Beside them, wedged in a fissure in the rock, was Justine Weaver's diary. Left with nothing at all, the family had set out to continue their journey on foot. The last entry was 25 December. When the diary was recovered and brought back to the fort, Colonel Bolt had read aloud the last extract at roll call. 'Without food we cannot carry on. All our strength is used up. So weak can barely walk. Do not expect to last another night . . . '

Glaze had forgotten how hungry he was. He slumped down in a pile of snow. Blades turned in his gut again and the glare of the sun scratched the back of his eyes. He stared at Justine Weaver's awkward script. When the family was on these flats, they had a wagon and supplies. Days later they were dead.

Glaze had nothing and he was too weak to stand. He slipped his hand inside his jacket and felt for the letter. Even though his fingers were numb, he managed to pull it out into the sunshine. As usual, the pages fell open along the fold. The maker's watermark was clear like an uncovered secret. Glaze's heart exploded in his chest. He flipped over page after page. Charlotte's copperplate had dissolved into a wide blue smear across each of them. Washed away by his soaking coat, every word had gone; nothing remained.

Glaze felt hollow; a great ache of despair engulfed him. If he had had strength, he would have cried out, he would have screwed up the paper and hurled it into the snow, he would have sobbed. He wanted to leap to his feet and yell and tear at the sky. Then his anguish tightened into a fist inside him; his rage turned to blame.

Not of himself; as he lay there in the snow he blamed Bolt. Glaze's thoughts crystallized; for the first time he saw everything clearly.

The colonel had ordered them up here knowing it was too late in the season. He was the one who made them take the High Trail; he was the one who insisted they take a supply wagon when the track was barely wide enough for a mule to pass; he was the one who ordered him to take a thief and a brawler from the lock-up, an old washed-up trail cook and a sergeant who could barely walk. It was no accident they had ended up like this. Bolt had ridden the High Trail himself; he knew what the weather could do. He knew what happened to the Weavers' party.

Since the incident on the plains, Bolt had held a grudge against him. Glaze knew that. Hard as it was, Glaze could accept demotion for the loss of his men; he had been the officer in charge and the decision to line up the troopers and go in alone had been his. He had made a mistake, one he would always carry on his conscience. He knew what he had done.

But Bolt hadn't believed him; that's what stuck in Glaze's craw. The colonel was affronted at the suggestion that one of the pioneers had shot a little Sioux girl in the back; he dismissed out of hand the account of Glaze being held at knifepoint and the idea that a Sioux brave allowed Glaze to live so he could give an account of what happened was too much for him. Bolt even suggested that Glaze realized what was happening, ran away and hid. Glaze had forced himself not to think about it; he hadn't allowed himself to believe that his commanding officer had got him pinned down under a boot heel of contempt. Now he knew it was true.

And then there was Charlotte. Glaze told her straight away about the demotion; she knew how he blamed himself for what happened. He hadn't hidden anything from her. Then the colonel had forbidden his daughter to have anything to do with him; he had sent her back to Boston without even giving them the chance to say goodbye.

Impossible questions echoed inside Glaze's head. Had Bolt really set the mission up to fail? Did he reckon on them returning to the fort at all? Did he think they would all starve up here? Is that what he intended to happen? By now, Glaze knew the answers. If he had allowed himself to think about it, he would have known all along.

Whatever it took, Glaze knew he had to get back to the fort. He had to confront Bolt. He deserved his rank reinstated. He was determined to see Charlotte again. As he stared across the plain of empty snow, Miller emerged from the trees with firewood in his arms. Glaze struggled to his feet and went to help him.

13

The two men stared into the blaze. Squares of animal skin Miller had cut from his hide lay in the embers at the edge of the fire. Snow drifted from the leaden sky and cloud began to press down on the plateau. Even with two of them working at it, collecting enough wood for a blaze had taken all day.

'Reckon we got enough to see us through?' Glaze eyed the pile of kindling and pine cones.

'Roasting us some deer hide,' Miller said.

He pointed to the squares of animal skin. The smell of the burning hair was sharp and disgusting.

'It ain't nightfall yet,' Glaze said. 'You've built up the fire too high.'

'Chew on this.' Miller gestured towards the squares of hide. His swollen face twisted into a smile. 'You won't feel hungry at all. I heard of a wagon train that got stuck in one of the high passes, survived a whole winter on deer hide.'

Glaze knew it wasn't true, but was grateful to Miller for trying to keep cheerful. Miller pulled the pieces of hide out of the embers on to the snow and flipped them over. Both sides were black and crisp.

'Only way you can eat this is if you boil it real slow,' Glaze said. 'As we ain't got a skillet, we're gonna have to chew it raw.'

'You can eat anything if you want to survive bad enough,' Miller said.

'I've heard the stories,' Glaze said, 'Just like everybody.'

He stared into the fire.

'Some of those wagon trains softened their belts in melted snow and ate 'em. Some of them wrapped their feet in rags and boiled up their boots.'

He looked at Miller.

'At least, that's what they thought they must have done when the search parties came across them the following spring.'

'Any of 'em survive?' Miller said.

All around them, snow was falling faster. Cloud closed over the plateau and dimmed the light. It was sometime between day and night; that's all they knew. Pretty soon the men would only be able to see a few feet in front of them. Snow had already settled on their shoulders.

'No,' Glaze said.

Miller looked away. He didn't want to look into the fire for comfort; he didn't want to catch Glaze's eye. Clouds of snow swirled round them; the wind snatched smoke from the fire, threw it in their faces and stung their eyes. On the edge of the flats, darkness thickened between the pines.

'Want me to cut you some of this hide?' Miller said. 'We ain't got nothing else.'

Glaze took out his knife, stabbed the charred piece of hide and held it up. The smell sickened him but he didn't remark on it. He stuffed it in his mouth. The first taste was of coal; chewing it exhausted him. The hide was too tough to bite through but if he held it on his tongue, he could suck out a taste of burned blood and putrid decay. He forced himself to keep the hide in his mouth; while he chewed, he battled to not make himself retch. He distracted himself by staring at the fire, forced himself to look at imaginary faces, examined the way the centres of the flames were blue, the way white ash crumbled at the ends of the sticks, looked at the way the blaze curled round the wood. He made himself concentrate on anything except the sickening flavour of rotten deer skin on his palate.

The inside of the deer skin round Glaze's shoulders was wet and stinking. Facing the fire, he struggled to make it into a cave around himself to shield him from the wind at his back. In front of him, the heat melted the frozen ground until he sat in a sea of mud. Above the fire, falling snow melted while it was still in the air and each gust of wind scattered him with rain.

Glaze spat out the lump of deer hide. He scooped up a handful of snow and gorged on it. Seeing this gave Miller the excuse he needed; he copied him. Both men spat into the fire, desperate to get rid of the filthy taste. They crammed more snow into their mouths, drew the hides round themselves and shifted close to the flames until their faces burned.

Darkness fell on them early. The wind gathered force, cried out, tore fistfuls of flame out of the fire, flung them away. The wood cracked and hissed and clouds of orange sparks exploded at them. Behind the men, the wind led the snow in a demented dance; at first it retreated, then charged full at them, hysterical and wild. Their faces burned, their backs froze. They pulled the deer hides over their heads.

'Should have shot him before he ate

the hard tack,' Miller said. 'Not afterwards.'

He meant it. His voice was hard and cynical. Glaze heard loathing for all officers in it, for every wrong decision, for every misguided order, for every loss. Most of all, Glaze heard contempt for him. He stared at the fire, too weak to defend himself. He didn't want to think about Miller's petty resentments or the way he despised authority.

'I said,' Miller leaned towards him to distract him from the fire, 'should have shot him before he ate the food.'

'Shut up, Miller.'

Glaze refused to look at him; he stared straight ahead into the flames. At least he was warm in front of the fire, inside the animal skin. The front of his jacket was almost dry and he was so used to the stink of the hide that it comforted him.

Miller grabbed a handful of snow and threw it at him. It spattered over Glaze's deer skin. Glaze ignored it.

'Why ain't you talking?' Miller said.

Glaze looked at him.

'We'll rest up by the fire,' Glaze said. 'We'll eat some more of this hide. We'll start down the wagon trail at first light.'

Miller threw a branch onto the fire. Flames tore through the dry pine needles.

'Why did you get picked for this mission, anyhow?' Miller said. 'I know why me and Schmidt got picked. We was in the lock-up and didn't have no choice.'

'To make up for the plains,' Glaze said. 'That's why.'

Miller stared at him.

'When everyone in your unit got killed?'

'The colonel said it would be a chance to redeem ourselves,' Glaze said coldly.

'Redeem ourselves?' Miller stared at Glaze as if he had just realized something. 'You stand to get promoted,' Miller said. 'That's it, isn't it?' Laughter scratched his throat. 'I'll bet you even volunteered for this.'

'The colonel ordered me here,' Glaze said.

'Officers. Every time it's the same,' Miller said.

'Shut up, Miller.'

Miller kicked the branches further into the fire. The flames reared in front of them.

'Knew it had to be something,' Miller said. 'I know they blamed you for the plains.'

'You're out of line, Private.'

Glaze struggled for some kind of dignity but there was no fight left in him. His words were empty and out of place.

'The men in the fort never blamed you,' Miller said. 'We talked about it. They thought you were lucky. The leader of that war party wanted a witness and he picked you.'

Glaze's brain lurched; he was hardly able to believe what he had heard. The men didn't blame him? He stared at Miller to see if this was some kind of wind up but it wasn't.

None of the officers had shown him sympathy over what happened on the plains. They had cold-shouldered him and sided with the colonel. In the Mess, he heard them mutter about the reputation of the regiment; he heard them talk loudly about patrols they had led, which had come back unscathed. When he tried to explain that the brave had held a knife to his throat, they refused to listen. When the colonel tore one of the bars off his shoulder and made him a lieutenant again, they said he got what he deserved.

Miller was waiting for his side of the story. Glaze looked into the private's wind-battered face; he had never spoken openly to an enlisted man.

'The colonel said I shouldn't have left the unit. Should have sent a trooper on ahead as a scout. That way I would have seen the attack coming and been able to defend against it.' He stared at the fire. 'That's all it was.'

Miller studied Glaze as he spoke. The skin had blackened on his cheeks and in places it was scraped raw where he had headed into the wind. Glaze avoided Miller's gaze.

'You lost your rank for that?' Miller said.

'The colonel wouldn't believe me about the Indian girl. He said no pioneer would shoot a child in the back, even if it was a Sioux.'

'Everyone knows some of them pioneers are so scared of the Sioux they reach for their rifles first and ask questions afterwards,' Miller said. 'That's what causes all the trouble.'

Glaze watched the flames devour the pine branches. The wind screamed at his back.

'Even if you had stayed with the unit, you couldn't have done nothing,' Miller went on. 'Once those braves got the jump on you, how were you supposed to stop them? Everyone knows those patrols need eyes in the back of their heads and half the time even that ain't good enough.'

'You know I was friends with the

colonel's daughter.' Glaze felt the words spill out of him as though a rock had cracked and a spring had burst through. 'We had an understanding.'

Glaze hesitated.

'Seen you reading the same letter over and over,' Miller said. 'That from her?'

Glaze didn't want to talk about this but the words were already in his mouth. He couldn't hold them back.

'Colonel's sent her back East. Told her to end it.'

Miller stared at him.

'He took away my rank because of the plains,' Glaze said. 'Now he's forbidden his daughter to have anything to do with me.'

'Forbidden?' Miller struggled to understand; it seemed ridiculous to him.

'Boston's a long way,' Glaze went on. 'It's a different world.'

'You'll do something grand and get yourself promoted again. Everything will turn out right.'

A dry laugh caught in Glaze's throat.

'She's a colonel's daughter,' Glaze said. 'Her pa reckons I ain't good enough.'

'And now he's sent us up here,' Miller said.

'He'll never change his mind,' Glaze went on. 'We started out with five. Only two of us left.'

'Officers.' Miller jerked his deer hide closer round him. 'We lost three men, we ain't got no food, the storm is raging and you're worried about a girl in Boston.'

Faces appeared in the fire in front of Glaze. Sometimes they were people he knew — old Newt Cobb, Bolt or officers from the fort. They stared at him curiously as if they were waiting to see what he would do until eventually the flames twisted them away. When Schmidt's face came, Glaze looked away and waited for it to disappear.

'Colonel was right.' Glaze stared at Miller. 'I shouldn't have left the men.'

'If you'd stayed with them you'd be dead now,' Miller said.

'By rights we should both be,' Glaze said. 'It was too late in the year for us to come up here.'

Glaze fell silent.

'You said you didn't volunteer?' Miller said.

'That's right.' Glaze shook his head.

'Did the colonel pick us as well?'

'Said it would be a chance for us to redeem ourselves.'

'Small party like this, season on the change,' Miller sounded puzzled. 'Ain't it usual for the commanding officer to ask for volunteers?'

'What are you saying?'

But Glaze already knew. Miller had reached the same unthinkable conclusion as he had. Bolt sent them up here knowing there was a good chance they wouldn't return. Needles of sweat jabbed inside Glaze's shirt. Bolt hadn't asked for volunteers; he knew the weather was against them; he had sent Charlotte away. He didn't care about the men: two troublemakers, an old cook and a sergeant who couldn't mount a horse without help. He wanted rid of them all.

Glaze watched the flames lurch and heard the despairing cry of the wind. Above him the snow raged on. When he looked round, Schmidt's body was already buried.

'What are you gonna do?'

Miller peered at him from under the deer hide. As he leaned forward and pushed the burned branches closer into the fire, flames blazed.

'Stay alive.'

Miller gave a husk of a laugh.

'And how do you aim to do that? Storm ain't about to blow over anytime soon, we ain't eaten for days and the way the snow has drifted we won't have the strength to get down off the mountain anyhow.'

Miller stared at him through a veil of falling snow.

'Looks to me like men have died because of some dispute between officers over some 'understanding' with a girl.'

He pulled the deer skin off his head

and faced Glaze. Snow caught in his hair. His skin was blistered and raw; his eyes blazed. His voice was steel.

'Seems to me the colonel don't want you for a son-in-law,' Miller spat. 'Between the two of you, you've got us all killed.'

'We ain't dead yet,' Glaze said. 'Anyhow, the only thing that matters is that we stay alive.'

He pushed himself to his feet, looked straight at Miller. He held out his hand to help him up.

'You know why those folks in the wagon train all died,' Glaze said. 'You know why that deer woman is still alive. You know what we've got to do.'

Miller threw another branch across the fire. A fist of sparks exploded between them.

Glaze took out his hunting knife. Neither of them looked over to where Schmidt's body lay.

'Did you hear me?' Glaze said. 'I'm saying we've got one chance and we've got to take it.'

Miller stared at up him. It took him a moment to work out what Glaze was saying. Orange firelight danced across Glaze's face.

'I can't do that,' Miller said slowly. He had come to a decision.

He waved Glaze's hand away and staggered to his feet on his own.

'Not to Schmidt.' Miller screwed up his face. 'Not to anyone.'

He turned in the direction of the entrance to the High Trail.

'I ain't staying here to watch you do that. I'll take my chances. The deer woman's probably brought up some of our supplies by now.'

Miller staggered as the shrieking wind barged into him.

'You won't make it,' Glaze tried to shout. 'It's too far.'

He watched Miller turn his back and stumble out of the ring of firelight into the darkness and the swirling snow.

'You've got to eat now or you'll die,' Glaze called after him.

But Miller probably didn't hear.

14

'Hey.'

A shout from somewhere echoed across the surface of the snow, a man's voice. Whether it was near or far away, Glaze couldn't tell. He couldn't even say if it was real or he had imagined it. He pushed back the deer hide covering him, brushed away the powdered snow that fell in his face and blinked at the grey morning light.

A line of smoke rose straight up from the ruins of the fire. The air was still, steel clouds pressed down and the light was thin. Snow was piled everywhere; there was no sign of a thaw. He listened again but doubted he had heard anything.

Then there was a movement at the far edge of the plateau. With the snow waist deep, he couldn't see anything. Glaze pulled himself from under the hide and sat up. Miller. He must have spent the night over there somewhere. Glaze's heart drummed. Then he noticed Miller's deerskin abandoned by the fire. Questions formed in his head but he couldn't say what they were.

Glaze shoved himself to his feet. Something was digging over by the entrance to the track. He fumbled for his Colt and tried to steady the gun with both hands but his arms were weak; his aim swerved. Snow glare stung the backs of his eyes. He tried to call out, but his voice barely scratched the air. He stumbled forward.

The sharp outline of a military hat flashed briefly above the line of snow. Glaze tried to call again, but the effort of trying to run was too much. His legs gave way; he staggered and fell. While he lay there and waited for his strength to gather, he heard someone blunder towards him through the snow.

Two arms reached down, grabbed him and hauled him up. Glaze struggled to focus.

'I thought you were dead,' Glaze said.

He stared up into the familiar face. It was Carey.

'Not yet, Lieutenant.'

Carey stared around at the sunlit plateau. The frozen surface glittered under the grey light; a furrow turned the drifts aside where his footsteps had ploughed through. Up ahead, the branches of the pines sagged under the weight of snow. The fire was burned out.

'Where's Schmidt?'

Glaze shook his head.

Carey stared at his feet. His shoulders dropped as if he was carrying a heavy weight.

'Found Miller at first light. Died in my arms.'

'What?' Glaze sank down in the snow. Not Miller, too.

'A hundred yards down the track,' Carey said. 'Looked as though he was trying to walk down the mountain. How d'you figure that?'

Glaze stared at Miller's deer hide thrown down in the snow.

Carey unhitched a pack wrapped in oilcloth from his shoulders and let it fall beside him.

'Brought some supplies.'

Glaze stared helplessly at him; it was too much to take in.

'Thought you were dead,' he repeated.

'Rockfall blocked the track,' Carey said. 'By the time I got across it you were so far ahead and the storm was so wild, I couldn't see any which way. Headed back to the cave.'

He looked at Glaze to make sure he was listening.

'The deer woman led me down to where the mules fell,' Carey said. 'Whole mountainside is crossed with cut-offs and she knows every one. If we'd had her with us from the start, we'd have been up here in no time.'

Glaze nodded.

'Knew you'd make it,' Carey went on. 'If the snow didn't blow you off the

205

path. Bet that food under that cairn tasted good.'

He saw Glaze stare at him empty-eyed.

'I'll make up the fire,' Carey said.

Later, they sat on the hides and stared at the flames. To Glaze the smell of coffee and frying bacon on the air was so wonderful as to be beyond comprehension. He fell on the bacon and crammed it into his mouth with both hands. With the first few mouthfuls, he felt his strength refueled. He licked the grease off his fingers when he'd finished.

'Told the deer woman I was coming up after you.' Carey took another slug of coffee. 'She showed me a cut-off through to the High Trail.'

Glaze cracked a piece of hard tack between his teeth.

'How come Miller was headed down the mountain like that?' Carey said. 'Didn't even have his deer skin round him. What could have made him forget that?'

Glaze broke the next piece of hard tack in his hand and let it soften in his coffee.

'His mind was gone when I got to him,' Carey reflected. 'Know what he said?'

Glaze reached for more hard tack.

'Don't let him eat me.' Carey shook his head and moved the coffee pot nearer the flames. 'Being up here with no food must have drove him crazy.'

Glaze didn't answer.

'If he could have hung on till you reached the cairn, he would have made it.' Carey swirled coffee round in his mug and stared into it.

'Guy as tough as Miller,' Carey went on. 'Something must have snapped in his head.'

Already past midday, the temperature dropped. No snow fell but lead clouds waited in the sky.

'Best start out,' Carey said. 'There's a cut-off we can take.'

As he climbed to his feet, the mound

of snow behind them caught his eye. He stared at it as if he was trying to work something out.

'Wait a minute.' Carey's words were barely a whisper. 'That Schmidt under there?'

Glaze looked away. He glanced at the fire; he scanned the place where the cairn stones were scattered; he stared out across the flats to the pines and beyond them at the bank of cloud, which hid the peaks. He looked anywhere except at Carey.

'Yeah.' Glaze coughed hard. 'That's him.'

'He made it up here?' Carey looked sick. 'I thought you meant the storm blowed him off the path.' His face tightened as he fought to understand. 'Took you a while to find the supplies under the cairn? He starved before you could get to 'em, is that it?'

Glaze hesitated.

'No,' he said. 'It wasn't like that.'

Carey waited for him to answer.

'What was it like?'

208

Glaze shook his head. 'Let's get moving.'

He pulled himself to his feet. Carey tied up the pack of supplies and slung it over his shoulders.

'I've known this guy I don't know how long,' Carey said.

He reached down and pulled back the hide that covered Schmidt's body. Carey stiffened; a question formed on his lips but no words came. Schmidt's eyes were closed and ice crystals froze in his beard; apart from livid patches of frostbite, his skin was china blue. The big man lay there in his grey army shirt; there was a neat, dark coin of frozen blood over his heart.

As Carey started to speak, something else caught his eye. Schmidt's jacket had been cut at the seam, slit down the length of the sleeve and folded back. Beneath it were knife marks on the bone where strips of flesh had been cut away from the arm. Carey stared at them for a while as though he couldn't see what they were. Then he looked back at the bullet hole in the chest. It took seconds for him to realize. He threw the hide over the corpse again and rounded on Glaze.

'You did this?' The words tore at his throat.

Carey fumbled clumsily for his gun. His hand shook; his fingers were stiff with cold. Glaze expected this; his Colt was already in his hand.

'You killed Schmidt so you could eat his flesh?'

Shock hollowed out Carey's voice. He sounded afraid. His face twisted as though the words tasted gross in his mouth.

'It wasn't like that,' Glaze implored him.

Carey struggled with his holster.

'I've seen what you did.' His voice shook. 'With my own eyes. That's what Miller meant, ain't it? He thought you were going to do the same to him so he ran off.'

'No,' Glaze said. 'That's not what happened.'

'He said, 'Don't let him eat me'. That's what he meant. He saw what you did to Schmidt.'

'No,' Glaze said. 'He ran off. He didn't want to stay up here.'

'He ran away. You were coming after him.' Carey was shaking. 'He died trying to escape.'

'Please,' Glaze begged. 'That ain't it.'

'You telling me you didn't eat . . . ' Carey screamed; then his voice faltered.

'Let me explain,' Glaze said.

'Court martial's too good for you,' Carey said.

'Schmidt stole the food,' Glaze said. 'He found it while we were asleep and ate it all. You know what he was like. He stole Miller's hard tack before.'

'Bull,' Carey pulled his gun out of his holster.

'I shot him. Court martial in the field. If you'd have been here you'd have agreed with me.'

'You're a liar,' Carey said.

'There was no food,' Glaze went on. 'There was no other choice if we wanted to stay alive.'

'You're lying.' Carey stared at him. 'What about Miller?'

'He wouldn't do it,' Glaze insisted. 'Look what happened.'

'I know these men,' Carey said. 'Miller never walked away from anything in his whole life. You're asking me to believe Schmidt ate an officer's rations right in front of him? Schmidt never disobeyed an officer since the day he enlisted.'

'You don't know what it was like up here,' Glaze pleaded with him.

'You expect me to believe you?' Carey's gun wavered in his hand. 'Colonel Bolt demoted you for cowardice. You led a patrol out on the plains and you were the only one to come back. Now you were looking to save yourself again. This time you pulled a gun and killed Schmidt, only when you turned on Miller, he ran off.'

Carey raised his Colt.

'I never held what happened on the

plains against you.' Carey's voice shook. 'I sure do now.'

Glaze fired. The clap of the pistol shot echoed over the snow and rolled away into the mountains. He holstered his gun and looked down at the sergeant's body, where it had fallen back into the snow. The eyes were surprised; Carey looked as if he was about to say just one more thing. His army Colt was still in his hand. A patch of blood was soaking through the front of his jacket. Glaze leaned down and brushed his hand over Carey's face to close his eyes.

Weak as he was, Glaze took Carey's body by the shoulders and dragged him so he lay beside Schmidt. Then he blundered through the snow in the direction Carey had come. It took him a long time to haul Miller's stiff corpse back to the others. He lined them up as respectfully as he could. Then he slumped back into a drift and stared at the three of them for a long time.

Glaze wanted to say some words but

none came. They were all tough men who had done their duty, he thought. That's the kind of thing he would be expected to say. That's the kind of thing Colonel Bolt would say to the lines of men on the parade ground back at the fort. He would talk about unflinching courage in the face of impossible odds and about the honour they brought to the regiment. His voice would be sombre and his expression grave.

Glaze knew different. Schmidt had been defeated by his own greed; Miller couldn't bring himself to do what he had to, to survive; blinded by belief in his men, Sergeant Carey had judged him wrongly. Some would say that it was too late for whys and wherefores and that none of that mattered now, but Glaze knew it did. It was the reason why he was alive and their cold bodies were lined up on the frozen ground. The other thing that mattered was that none of them should have been sent on this mission in the first place. They had all been betrayed; Glaze was the only one left who could get to the heart of that for them.

A ceiling of cloud pressed down on the flats. Within an hour, visibility would be gone. Glaze added a bundle of kindling to Carey's pack of supplies. He took a last look at the bodies of the men. By nightfall they would be frozen.

Doubtless, a patrol would make the climb up from the fort to recover the remains in the spring. Glaze would make sure he rode with them. As he swung the pack of supplies onto his shoulder and headed in the direction of the track, a cold wind swept snowflakes down through the air.

15

Three Weeks Later.

A patrol picked Glaze up in the foothills. They saw the smoke from his fire from some way off but when they got close they mistook him for a trapper who had made his way down from the peaks before winter finally closed in. He was half-starved, dressed in the ragged remains of a uniform with his boots split down the seams. His beard was wild; patches of frostbite blackened his face and fingers. An uncured, stinking deer hide, which he clutched to his shoulders together with a few army rations had kept him alive.

As they approached Fort Brandish, Glaze's snow blindness kicked in. The troopers bandaged his eyes with cotton torn from a shirt, sat him on a horse and led him across the plain and through the gates. He didn't see that the parade ground flag flew at half mast.

The fort doctor prescribed food and rest for Glaze and advised the camp commander to hold off the debrief. He said Glaze's sight would return provided his eyes remained bandaged for a while; he undertook to keep a daily check on the frostbite. Glaze ate a week's worth of rations in one sitting then slept in a bunk in the infirmary for three days straight. On the fourth day, the camp sawbones removed the bandages from his eyes and amputated two frostbitten fingers from his left hand. On the fifth, Glaze was summoned to the Command Room.

Major Fairburn stared out of the window across the parade ground where the various units were falling in for evening roll call. The stove was lit and the room was comfortably warm. Glaze sat in a padded leather chair with his hand bandaged and his arm in a sling. He listened to Fairburn describe the riding accident that had killed Colonel Bolt.

'Cavalry man through and through,' Fairburn reflected. 'Put that stallion through his paces the first time he took him out. Should have spent some time getting to know him first; the horse didn't take kindly to being pushed so hard by a new rider. When he threw him, the colonel broke his neck straight off.'

Fairburn turned to face Glaze.

'If the colonel could have chosen a way to go,' he went on, 'I guess being thrown from his mount at full gallop would have been it. Nothing he liked better than to lead a charge.'

Fairburn drew up a chair on the opposite side of the stove.

'I'm just glad his daughter wasn't here when it happened.'

Glaze felt himself colour at the mention of Charlotte.

'Anyhow,' Fairburn said, 'that leaves me in command of Brandish until the brass decides what to do. I'd better hear what you've got to say.'

Fairburn stretched his legs out to catch the heat from the stove and settled back in his chair.

Glaze told him everything. He recounted the mission as if he were reading from a diary. No detail was left out. As the narrative went on, Fairburn leaned forward and watched Glaze closely.

'So you didn't see hide nor hair of the Crowleys?' Fairburn said when Glaze finished speaking.

'Not a trace,' Glaze said. 'The woman we met on the mountain told us they'd all left before we got there. Guess they'll be back in the spring when the wagon trains pass through again. Best chance we've got of catching them is to wait until then.'

Fairburn got up from his chair and crossed over to the window. It was dark now. He stared out into the empty parade ground. Cold, wet moonlight lit the mountain peaks. When he turned back to face Glaze, he shook his head as if he was trying to decide something.

'Hard to figure why the colonel ordered this mission in the first place.' Fairburn looked puzzled. 'Any suggestions?'

Glaze wanted to say that Colonel Bolt had misjudged him over what happened on the plains; that he blamed him and had never forgiven him for it. He wanted to say that he wanted rid of him, that he chose men he regarded as expendable to ride with him and that he knew the High Trail was too narrow for a wagon to pass. He wanted to say that the colonel resented him because his daughter liked him. Most of all, he wanted to say that Bolt had set the mission up to fail; he was guilty of treachery.

'No, sir,' Glaze said. 'Can't think of any.'

His answer didn't seem to satisfy Major Fairburn.

'Well, I can,' Fairburn said.

He turned back to the window.

'One thing you can say about the

colonel, he always put the reputation of the regiment first. When he received his commission, the army was all about honour and glory. He always wanted to be the one who led the charge. Now times have changed; what we try to do is keep the peace and protect the pioneers.'

Fairburn crossed the room and knelt to riddle the stove. He shoved in another log and slammed the iron door shut.

'He was right about the reputation of the regiment, though. A regiment that is well thought of thinks well of itself; morale is high and the men get the job done.'

He paused to see if Glaze followed him.

'Ordinarily,' Fairburn went on, 'I'd require you to write a report of the mission.'

He sat back in the chair opposite Glaze.

'I respect the fact that you did what you had to. You succeeded in staying alive where circumstances were impossible. You did your duty and you did your best; you're a brave man. I want the regiment to know and I want them to respect you for it. For that reason I shall recommend that your captain's rank is reinstated.'

'Sir . . . ' Glaze was winded. For a moment he couldn't believe what he had heard.

'I'm grateful . . . ' Glaze began. Surprise and delight sang in his blood; he couldn't find the right words.

Fairburn raised his hand. He didn't want Glaze's thanks.

'There is something I want you to do in return.'

Glaze leaned forward.

'Some of the things that happened, some of the things you did,' Fairburn lowered his voice confidentially, 'are best not spoken of. I want your word as an officer that you will never mention the circumstances of how the men died.' He paused and stared hard at Glaze. 'Nothing is to be gained by turning the fort into a rumour mill. You will simply say that they were brave men who did their duty honourably. You will say they faced impossible odds with courage, and that the mission you were all engaged on was a success. The proof of this will be your promotion. After all, you completed the mission and delivered a report to your commanding officer in person.'

'Sir.'

Glaze sat back in his chair and let the heat from the stove soak into him. His hand throbbed mercilessly; spots of blood appeared on the white bandage and pain drained his strength. He had returned to the fort prepared to face down Bolt, ready to risk a court martial, ready to tell the truth. He had wanted Bolt to take responsibility, to admit what he had done. But with Bolt gone, everything was different.

Fairburn knew what they had been through, he understood why Glaze had done the things he had. He recommended him for promotion; when that word was inside his head, pride warmed Glaze like a fire.

'I know that you can keep a confidence,' Fairburn smiled at him. 'I shall send off my recommendation in the morning.'

Fairburn left Glaze by the stove and leafed through a pile of papers on the desk. Glaze remembered how Colonel Bolt used to perch there like a bird of prey. Fairburn picked up an envelope sealed with red wax and stamped with the regimental seal.

'There is one more thing,' he said.

He held out the vellum envelope for Glaze to read the words, 'Miss Charlotte Bolt' written there.

'This is the official notification of Colonel Bolt's death. I wrote it myself. I understand that the young lady lives with an aunt in Boston. I've held off sending it because to have an army courier turn up on your doorstep and receive such a letter would be a mighty hard thing.'

Fairburn handed the letter to Glaze.

'I want you to take it,' Fairburn said. 'I want you to deliver the news in person. It's the least the regiment can do.'

'I became acquainted with Miss Bolt during the summer,' Glaze said.

Fairburn nodded. 'Better she receives the news from someone she knows.'

Glaze slipped the letter into his inside pocket and got to his feet.

'There's a unit heading East in the morning,' Fairburn went on. 'You can ride the first hundred miles with them; after that you can make your own way. When you get to Boston, spend some time there. Take some leave. You need to rest up after what you've been through. Give your hand time to heal.'

He nodded to show that Glaze was dismissed and returned Glaze's salute.

'Captain Glaze,' he said matter-of-factly.

Hearing the words as he turned smartly on his heel, Glaze failed to control the grin that lit his face.

★　★　★

Next morning, as golden dawn light burst over the plains to the east, a unit was mounted up and ready to ride out at the fort gate. The air was sharp and still; the cobalt night sky retreated over the mountains in the west. The horses stamped and shifted, restless to be on their way; their breath hung in misty clouds in front of their faces.

Glaze rode alongside the captain at the head of the column. His arm was strapped tightly to his chest with a fresh bandage; if his hand hurt, he barely noticed it. His mind was on the weeks of hard riding ahead of him, from fort to fort down the Emigrant Road until he reached Independence. After that, the journey would be easier; he might even be able to send word ahead to let Charlotte know he was on his way.

Major Fairburn acknowledged the column as it moved out. He caught Glaze's eye and nodded respectfully. Fairburn understood what Bolt had

226

done; he knew what Glaze had gone through; he knew and he had given Glaze back his rank. Glaze wanted to thank him but even if he could find the words, it was not the army way. Glaze saluted smartly. He thought of Charlotte's name inscribed on the envelope in his saddle-bag; he thought of the long trail stretching ahead. He would not see the major or the fort again until spring.

THE END

We do hope that you have enjoyed reading this large print book.

Did you know that all of our titles are available for purchase?

We publish a wide range of high quality large print books including:
Romances, Mysteries, Classics
General Fiction
Non Fiction and Westerns

Special interest titles available in large print are:
The Little Oxford Dictionary
Music Book, Song Book
Hymn Book, Service Book

Also available from us courtesy of Oxford University Press:
Young Readers' Dictionary
(large print edition)
Young Readers' Thesaurus
(large print edition)

For further information or a free brochure, please contact us at:
Ulverscroft Large Print Books Ltd.,
The Green, Bradgate Road, Anstey,
Leicester, LE7 7FU, England.
Tel: (00 44) 0116 236 4325
Fax: (00 44) 0116 234 0205

MISSOURI VIGILANTES

Mark Bannerman

General Sherlock has issued an order to exterminate the bandits of Taney County: shoot them like animals and hang all prisoners. So when sixteen-year-old Billy Stark falls into a trap and attempts to steal an army payroll, the military are hot on his trail. Fleeing for his life and burdened by a wounded companion, Billy faces extreme peril and is lured into a world where lynching, torture and bullets have replaced the law. Striving to maintain his morality, Billy finds himself drawn deeper into a web of evil . . .

HORSE SOLDIER'S RETURN

James Del Marr

Bounty hunter Horse Soldier returns from Navajo country to find his wife and daughter, Sarah and Clementine, have been kidnapped. But Cal Livermore doesn't want money: he wants Horse Soldier, in revenge for the shooting of his brother Laramie Pete. Forging a partnership with Running Deer McVicar, who is in pursuit of his father's killer, Horse Soldier sets out on the renegades' trail — but will they rescue Sarah and Clemy in time?

SHE WORE A BADGE

Steve Hayes

Ten-year-old Hope Corrigan is out sketching in the New Mexico brush when she runs across Deputy Marshal Liberty Mercer: a woman as handy with a Colt .45 as with a Winchester '86, and on the trail of three escaped convicts. When Hope's father is murdered by the criminals, leaving her orphaned, the marshal takes her under her wing as they continue the pursuit. But along the way, they must forge an uneasy alliance with bandit Latigo Rawlins, an old acquaintance of Mercer's — and killer of her dear friend and comrade . . .

DROVER'S BOUNTY

J. L. Guin

Drover Sam Hall is accused of cheating at cards by gunslinger J.D. Seldon — and in the ensuing scuffle, both J.D. and Sam's friend Daniel are shot dead. After collecting the $500 bounty on J.D.'s head, Sam sets off in pursuit of Daniel's killer. But J.D.'s half-brother Ben is also bent on revenge, and has issued his own bounty on Sam. With gunslingers and hardcases dogging Sam's every move, there is only one way out of this situation. He must find, and face down, Ben Seldon . . .

ROGUE SOLDIERS

Corba Sunman

Army investigator Captain Slade Moran is hunting the killer of an officer when he rides into Grey Ridge, having lost the trail of the fugitive. Fresh orders await him at Fort Grant, where he finds a hornets' nest of trouble. There has been a spate of inexplicable desertions, trouble between the troopers and townspeople, and a young lieutenant has been court-martialled and cashiered for embezzlement — though his commanding officer doubts his guilt. Moran is up against unscrupulous men, vicious killers, and a rogue soldier . . .

SHARPER'S QUEST

Jay D. West

Sharper Wade rides into Virginia City more by chance than intent. He'd heard about the Comstock Lode and its vast quantities of gold and silver, but his own concerns are limited to feeding himself and his horse. When he intervenes in a brutal attack on a defenceless girl and her grandfather by three cow-boys, he ends up in jail accused of murder. But a witness exonerates him — freeing Sharper to set out on the killers' trail . . .